Cupid's Silver Spark

A Bangers Tavern Romance Novella

Sadira Stone

Cupid's Silver Spark

♥

Will Cupid's misfire cost her everything?

Still stinging from a breakup, Carla Portofino wants nothing to do with Valentine's Day. When her bestie drags her to Bangers Tavern's Anti-Valentine's Bash, Cupid gifts her a swoonworthy silver fox. Maybe a no-strings fling is the remedy for her tattered heart? He seems perfect, until his company makes a grab for her building, tangling them in more string than either can handle.

All Jeremy Franklin wants on Valentine's Day is to escape the lovey-dovey hype. But his best friend insists on cheering him up with a trip to Bangers Tavern, where Jeremy meets Carla, a woman so tempting he simply must pursue her. Trouble is, his real estate firm has the hots for her building, and he'll have to fight to save her shop from their greedy grasp.

To keep her business, Carla must dare the hardest hurdle of all—trust the enemy. Will her silver fox prove a predator, or will Cupid's arrow strike true?

Copyright

♥

QUALITY CONTROL: I strive to produce error-free books, but even with all the critique partners, beta readers, and editors, sometimes an error slips through. Pretty please, if you find a typo or formatting issue, let me know at sadirastoneauthor@gmail.comso I may correct it. Thank you!

Dedication

♥

To Duncan, my HEA
  And to my readers
  May your tots be crispy
  and your love stories steamy!

Contents

Valentine's Day

♥

"I'm sure your girlfriend will love it."

Wincing just the tiniest bit, Carla Portofino added the finishing touches to the gift box—a pouf of scarlet ribbon curlicues and a glittery Vintage Rapture sticker. Inside lay the antique, lace-trimmed chemise she'd been eyeing all week. She promised herself if it was still on the mannequin by the end of her Valentine's sale, she would take it home. But right before closing time, this cute, thirty-something guy snapped it up for his lucky sweetheart.

Business is business. No sense moping about it.

She tightened the knot, tucked a silk rose under the ribbon, and handed the package to the customer. "Happy Valentine's Day, hon."

His grin could've lit a skyscraper. "Thanks, ma'am. Same to you."

Ouch.

She gave herself a mental shake. Ma'am was a perfectly polite way to address a grown woman, and at forty-five, she certainly was grown. No need to infer that he found her old. Ancient. Decrepit.

The brass bell above the shop door tinkled, and her best friend sailed through.

"All done?" Shari fluffed her shoulder-length hair, copper-penny red this week, and glanced around. "Dang, girl! Looks like a tornado swept through here." She poked through the display table near the door. "You sold all those crystal perfume bottles? Too bad. I was gonna buy one."

Carla leaned on the glass counter and sighed. "Thank God this Valentine's Day ordeal is over. I'm beat. You?"

"Same. Been styling hair and painting faces all day. My dogs are barkin'." She lifted a sampler bottle of Love Goddess cologne and gave her cleavage a spritz.

Carla reached for her keys. "Wanna come over? We can get pizza and watch a horror movie."

Shari wrinkled her freckled nose. "Shut your blasphemous mouth. It's Valentine's Day."

"My point exactly." Dumped right before Valentine's Day. How cliché. Until a few days ago, she thought that only happened in rom-coms.

The doorbell tinkled again, and a cute young dude in brown coveralls entered, holding a large box. "Delivery for Carla Portofino?"

Shari ogled him as Carla signed for the package.

"What is it?"

"Probably just something green for St. Patrick's Day." Decorating for each holiday and curating merchandise to match gave her an edge over the other vintage shops up and down Tacoma's Sixth Avenue, an eclectic neighborhood of funky boutiques, restaurants, bars, and weed dispensaries. Considering the shop's narrow frontage, she needed every advantage. Competition was tough on The Ave., and six feet of glass was all she had to lure shoppers inside her jewel box filled with gorgeous garments, wearable art, whimsical decorations, and other sparkly delights. Unlike her competitors' jumbled, musty shops, Carla's boutique was arranged to pamper customers with velvet benches, baroque-framed mirrors, sweet scents, and a dish of foil-wrapped chocolates beside the till.

Shari snatched up one of her favorite bonbons from the crystal bowl. "Aren't you gonna open your package?"

"Okay, Ms. Nosey-pants." Carla slit the packing tape, lifted the lid, and groaned.

"What, they got your order wrong?" Shari asked around a mouthful of candy.

"It's my stuff from Xavier's place." After three years together, her boyfriend announced last week he'd found someone new, and that was that. Okay, maybe they weren't technically living together, and no promise of a shared future had been made, but their lives were so enmeshed, she'd naturally assumed what they had would last. Which was monumentally stupid. Even his name started with X. Huge red flag.

She lifted a pink envelope embossed with hearts. "And he sent me a Valentine's Day card."

"The bastard! What does it say?"

Carla handed it over, and Shari read aloud, "Wishing you lots of love in your future. It's been an honor knowing you. Take care." She screwed up her face. "That's it?"

"Guess so." Head pounding, jaws vise-tight, Carla smacked the counter. "I've changed my mind. I want an action movie. With explosions. Lots of explosions."

Shari gave a dismissive wave. "Screw that nonsense. We're going out."

"On Valentine's Day? How depressing."

"Not necessarily." Shari bustled around the shop, grabbing supplies—a pair of jeweled hair combs, a velvet scarf in glowing scarlet, and the cologne sampler. With a tuck here, a fluff there, and a generous spritz of Love Goddess, she primped Carla until she sparkled.

"Amazing." Carla checked her reflection in the gilt-framed mirror. "You'd never know I've been on my feet since six this morning."

"Wimp. I've been up since five. Come on. We're going to Bangers."

"The bar up the street?"

Shari's grin glittered with the promise of shenanigans. "Tonight they're having an Anti-Valentine's party. It'll be fun!"

"I don't know, Shar. I'd rather just chill."

"They have tater tots," Shari coaxed in a sing-song voice.

Carla rolled her eyes. "Oh, all right. One hour." She locked the shop, bundled up against the icy wind, and followed her friend up Sixth Avenue.

Couples, couples, everywhere! Cramming the restaurants and bars, strolling hand in hand, stopping to smooch while blocking the goddamn sidewalk as if they were the only people in the whole wide universe. Clutching her vintage swing coat, Carla grumbled and sidestepped an amorous, giggling pair.

"C'mon, slowpoke," Shari called over her shoulder.

"I'm trying." She dodged a scruffy guy hawking cellophane-wrapped roses outside Jazzbones. With a prickle of alarm, she noted a new business where a used record shop had been just last week—yet another gastropub advertising twenty dollar "small plates."

"Damn yupsters," she muttered. "Stay in your own neighborhood. Leave mine alone."

Shari shot her an impatient glance. "What are you grumbling about?"

"Gentrification. Look at this." She tapped the next new shop window. "A hundred dollars for a baby jacket?"

"Life is change, sweetie. You can't fight it."

They approached Bangers Tavern, a low-slung, brick-front building with green and white striped awnings. Shouts, laughter, and the scent of fried food drifted out.

"Now this is more like it, right?" Shari pointed to the window mural, an aerial battle resembling a WWI dogfight, but with chubby winged archers instead of biplanes. At the bottom, a cupid lay on its back with X's for eyes and its feet up like a dead bug.

Carla couldn't help grinning at the image that perfectly captured her current attitude toward romance. She reached for the door, but the ginormous bouncer beat her to it, releasing a beer-scented wall of heat and noise. The bar was packed with revelers. Good to know she wasn't the only one sick of the obnoxious, lovey-dovey Valentine's hype.

"Evening, ladies. Welcome to Bangers." The man mountain inclined his shiny, shaved head. "Five-dollar cover charge tonight. Fundraiser for Tacoma Domestic Violence Shelter."

Shari handed him cash, then tugged Carla inside. Giggling, she glanced back at the entrance. "Isn't he luscious?"

"Sure, if you like 'em big and brawny."

Shari growled like a cougar with a bad chest cold. "That's just how I like 'em."

Rolling her eyes, Carla unfastened her coat. "We're not here to pick up guys, are we? Because honestly, I'd rather clean my gutters than make small talk tonight."

"Calm down, Miss Cranky-Pants. Maybe a drink will improve your sense of humor."

They elbowed their way through the raucous crowd—mostly on the younger side, thanks to the college just a dozen blocks away. Carla's faux fur-trimmed coat, satin blouse, and mid-century rhinestone jewelry were perfect for her work persona as Queen Magpie, but here among the Puget Sound University hoodies, she stood out like a flashy peony in a field of daisies. She raised her voice over the booming music. "Should've gone home first and changed into something more casual."

"Why?" Shari gave her a hip bump. "You're a gorgeous woman. Own your hotness."

The bearded blond bartender flashed a killer smile. "What can I get you, Your Hotness?"

Heat painted Carla's cheeks.

Shari leaned her elbows on the bar and batted her eyelashes like some cartoon femme fatale. "What's the special, darlin'?" Carla's bestie left Alabama when she was twelve, but she pulled her Southern drawl out of mothballs whenever she was feeling frisky—or drunk.

Pretty Bartender Boy ticked off on his long fingers. "We got the Black Heart, a Bourbon Sour-on-Love, a Dark 'n' Stormy, a Blue Valentine, and the Suffering Bastard."

Carla ordered the Sour-on-Love, perfect for her current mood. With smooth grace, the young man mixed, shook, poured, and slid their drinks across the bar. Shari stuffed a ten into his jar.

"Thanks, pretty lady." He inclined his tousled head toward the low staircase that led to the pool tables and dartboards. "Be sure and try the shooting gallery. Hit Cupid's ass and win a drink token."

"We're on it, sugar." With a wink, Shari looped her arm through Carla's. "Ever think about dating a younger guy?" she asked as they wove through the crowd. "Might do you good."

Carla coughed out a bitter laugh. Who needed that kind of pressure? She was already feeling insecure after Xavier kicked her to the curb. But it was nice to be noticed, like a vitamin tonic for her ego. Tonight, she'd enjoy whatever attention came her way, then go home alone. Because dating was like the delicious, tart cocktail in her hand—fun to indulge in now and then, but imbibing too much could wreck you.

"This way." Shari yanked Carla's arm. "Let's shoot Cupid's ass."

"Easy now, don't spill my drink."

Shari didn't, but the blue-haired, tattooed server almost did. "Sorry, ladies," she chirped. She gave Carla a quick up and down glance. "Love your jewels. Très chic." Hoisting her tray, she sashayed into the mob, the scent of tater tots trailing behind her.

Carla's stomach rumbled. "Can't we skip Cupid and eat?"

"Shoot first, tots second." Shari paid the grizzled old guy manning the dart boards, now covered with cartoon Cupids. Gripping her plastic dart gun, she assumed a TV cop stance. "Just imagine that plump, pink ass is Xavier's." She squinted and fired, missing the target entirely.

"Amateur." Carla turned her right side to the target, raised the dart gun, quieted her breath, and fired.

"Bullseye!" the old guy hooted. "You a cop, Miss?"

She blew on the plastic muzzle before handing it over. "I'm a vintage fashionista."

"Remind me not to mess with you." He handed her a drink coupon. "Stick around for the piñata at ten. Dawn stuffed some good prizes in there."

"Will do, thanks." She turned to Shari. "Now can we eat? Customers kept me running all day. Had to skip lunch."

Her friend snapped a salute. "Yes ma'am, Annie Oakley."

Carla scanned the bar, but every table was taken. "Maybe we should get dinner to go?"

"Oh no. You're not wiggling out that easy. We'll just share with someone. C'mon."

Drinks held high, they skirted the dance floor where a gaggle of women their age were bouncing to Pink's "So What?" beneath a kitschy disco ball. Sure enough, a grinning Cupid piñata dangled over the low stage. Interspersed with twinkle lights, paper hearts in pink, red, and purple fluttered from the ceiling. More lay scattered on the tables.

Shari elbowed her and pointed. "Over there, by the window. Cute, aren't they?"

Carla groaned.

At a tall, tiny table, a pair of forty-ish men gesticulated over beer glasses, their heads inches apart. The bearded one looked up, grinned, and nudged his friend.

"You ladies looking for a spot? We don't mind sharing. Right, Jer?"

The other man raised his head, and time slowed. The din stilled. The crowd blurred.

"Which one you want?" Shari asked. "Tall, dark, and yummy, or the silver fox?"

Carla's mouth opened, but no sound emerged.

Squaring her shoulders, Shari strutted forward. "Mighty kind of y'all to offer. My friend here is famished. If we don't get her some tater tots soon, she just might expire."

"That would be a damn shame." The fox's slow smile simmered with sexy mischief. The silver at his temples proved he was experienced enough to deliver. Crinkles at the corners of his dark eyes deepened as he aimed his intense gaze at Carla.

Mayday!

"Miss Rosie," he called without breaking the stare. "We've got a tot emergency here."

The blue-haired server bopped up to their table. "Tonight's specials are Love Bites, AKA jalapeno poppers with bacon, or Diego's famous tots with cheesy artichoke dip and bacon."

Shari tittered. "Because what cures a broken heart better than bacon?"

The server nodded, her curls bouncing. "It's a proven fact."

"Bring us a double order of each," the fox said. "That is, if you ladies don't mind sharing."

Right then, Carla wouldn't mind sharing all sorts of things with him—her phone number, her bed, her deepest fantasies...

Must be the bourbon talking. She told the server, "And an iced tea, please."

"Bullshit," Shari interjected. "You're not spending your hard-won drink coupon on brown water." She snatched the ticket and dropped it onto the server's tray. "Darlin', bring whichever of those cocktail specials you like best."

Carla opened her mouth to object, but Shari shot her a don't-mess-with-me glare.

Chuckling, the dark-haired guy introduced himself. "Leo Delgado. And this is Jeremy Franklin."

"Shari Poulsen. And this is my bestie, Carla Portofino."

Jeremy. Carla mentally rolled the name over her tongue as they shook hands all around. *A friendly name. Down to earth. Kinda sexy, in an approachable way.*

"So," Shari sipped her drink. "What brings you boys here tonight?"

Leo elbowed his friend. "Mr. Grump-ass here was going to spend the evening watching Netflix alone. Figured a party would do him good."

Carla ignored Shari's pointed stare and kept her focus on Jeremy. "What were you going to watch?"

He shrugged, but the corners of his mouth ticked upward. "Maybe a disaster movie. Seems suitable for the occasion." He inclined his head toward his friend. "Mr. Party Monster wouldn't leave me in peace. I figured a few drinks would shut him up." His smile widened. "Now I'm glad I surrendered." He scooted a little closer and nudged Carla with his arm. "How about you?"

A flush of warmth spread from the contact, and the room tilted just a tiny bit.

"Tots," she declared, a preemptive strike before Shari spilled any embarrassing details of her pathetic love life. "I hear this place has the best in Tacoma."

"It's true." Jeremy sipped his drink. "The chef here is some kind of cosmic tot master."

"Obi Wan Tater Tot," his friend agreed.

A moment later their server deposited proof: a platter heaped high with golden nuggets of crispy potato goodness, smothered in hot, cheesy artichoke dip and garnished with bacon folded into hearts.

"Oh look," Shari chirped, "there's a bacon heart for each of us." She grabbed one and held it to her lips. "C'mon, guys. Let's break some hearts." She did so with a chomp.

Jeremy slid the platter toward Carla. "After you."

She scooped tots onto her plate and, holding Jeremy's gaze, crumbled her bacon heart over the top.

"I like your style." He passed the basket of jalapeño poppers before snapping his bacon heart neatly in half.

Self-conscious about eating while those dark eyes followed her every move, Carla dug in. The combination of crunchy tots and creamy artichoke dip with a spicy kick was pure heaven. She closed her eyes and released a moan of pleasure. When she opened them again, she found Jeremy still watching her, a flush across his cheekbones, his lips softly parted.

Yikes!

She kept her gaze on her plate and off Mr. Smolder. Meanwhile, Shari and Leo chattered about everything and nothing until Beyonce's "Single Ladies" blasted over the speakers. Shari grabbed her wrist. "C'mon, Carla. Let's dance!"

The bar's miniscule dance floor was already packed, and the last time Carla dove into a crowd like this one, she got an elbow to the head. The black eye took weeks to disappear.

She offered a weak smile. "I'll pass."

Leo didn't need prompting. "I'll dance with you, pretty lady." And off they went. Over her shoulder, Shari pointed to Jeremy and flashed a thumbs-up.

"Sorry." Carla wiped her greasy lips and gave Jeremy a sheepish grin. "My friend's got matchmaking on her mind."

His gaze rose from her lips to her eyes. "And you're not keen?"

"Just got out of a relationship. I'm not eager to dive back in yet."

He offered her the last jalapeño. When she waved it away, he popped it into his mouth. The working of his jaw muscles was mesmerizing.

Good Lord, he even chews sexy.

"Well," he intoned in a rumbly voice, "whoever let you go is a Class A idiot."

Heat painted her cheeks. "I'm inclined to share your opinion, but hey, if he doesn't want me, I don't want him either."

"Good attitude." His hand closed over hers—his warm, heavy, callused hand. He must do some kind of physical labor. His tan complexion suggested lots of outdoor time, but the fabric and tailoring of his dress shirt and dark jeans bespoke the big bucks that came from office work.

"You from Tacoma, Jeremy?"

"Born and raised. You?"

"I live down by Wright Park." *Why are you telling him where you live?*

"I'm in Old Town. What brings you to Bangers, besides your matchmaking friend?"

"My shop is just up the street. Vintage Rapture."

He tilted his head and rubbed the dimple in his square chin. "Hmm. Don't think I've seen that one."

"Most of my clientele is female. Though lots of guys visited the shop this past week to buy gifts for their sweethearts. How about you?"

"No sweetheart to buy for."

"I figured as much, since you're here with Leo and he's busy flirting with my friend."

He flushed again.

"I meant, what kind of work do you do?"

"Ah. I'm in real estate."

Ho hum. Still, she didn't want to ruin the flirtatious vibe between them, a balm on her bruised heart. "Must be fun peeking into people's homes. You can tell a lot about a person by their private space."

"I suppose you can. I'm more on the commercial side of the business."

"Office buildings?"

"And retail spaces." He pulled a shiny embossed business card from his breast pocket. "Give me a call if you ever want to look for a new location."

"Nope. I like where I am just fine." But she pocketed his card all the same because...well, he was cute.

The music cut off, and Dawn O'Malley, owner of Bangers Tavern, mounted the low stage. She'd decked herself out in pink and red from the tips of her sparkly short locs to the toes of her bedazzled Chuck Taylors.

"Y'all having fun?" she called into the mic.

Carla clapped and hooted along with the rest of the crowd. Dawn came into her shop from time to time in search of gifts for her nieces. One of these days, she'd convince her to buy something for herself—in fact, she had a purple velveteen biker jacket that would suit Dawn's cheeky personality.

Dawn consulted her clipboard. "Next up, our worst first date competition. Last chance to sign up. We've got some really nice prizes for folks willing to share their dating disasters."

Jeremy nudged Carla's arm. "You signed up?"

She shook her head. Actually, she'd never had a really horrible first date. Boring ones, yes, but nothing awful enough to win tonight's prize. The bad part always came later when the guy lost interest.

Carla scanned the crowd for Shari. No sign of her. She turned to Jeremy. "Can you see your friend anywhere?"

He stood and peered into the mob. "Over there, by the photo booth."

Sure enough, Shari was vamping for the camera, a feather boa around her neck and a tiara atop her fiery hair. Leo popped a top hat on his head and joined her, snapping selfie after selfie.

"Typical Shari," Carla muttered. Her friend burned through cute guys at a rate that would decimate Carla's bruised heart. If only she could adopt Shari's easy come, easy go attitude, she'd be a much happier person.

Turning back to Jeremy, she found him nibbling his lower lip. *Oh Lord, please don't ask me to take pictures with you.*

Instead, he nodded toward the dance floor. A slower song had chased most of the dancers away. "You know, Leo will give me a mountain of shit if I don't ask you to dance." His eyebrows flicked up, his dark gaze playful. "Help me out?"

Across the crowd, Carla caught Shari's eye. Her friend made a shooing gesture and mouthed, "Go!"

She huffed a sigh. Cozying up to this gorgeous man would just mess with her head. She didn't need that kind of distraction right now. On the other hand, she'd never see him again after tonight, so why not indulge?

"Sure. Let's dance."

While Beyoncé crooned about the best thing she never had, Jeremy grasped Carla's hand in his broad, warm one and led her to the dance floor. In her tall boots, her chin came just to his shoulder, the perfect height for snuggling close. But he held her at a gentlemanly distance, a few inches of heated air between their swaying bodies. He smelled like an old-fashioned men's club—bourbon, tobacco, and leather.

Unlike Xavier, who could never quite find the beat, Jeremy moved her in flawless rhythm with the music. The mirrored ball overhead dappled them with rainbow-hued light. His heat, his probing gaze, the firm curve of his shoulder beneath her hand—it was enough to make a girl lose her head. And then, *heaven help me*, he started humming along, his rich baritone a deep counterpoint to Beyoncé's soaring high notes. A helpless moan escaped her lips.

He tipped his head so his cheekbone rested against her temple. "That bad, huh?"

"No, you have a lovely voice." Her guard loosened by strong drink and strong, luscious man, she nestled closer.

He sucked in a breath, then released a sigh that stirred her hair. His long fingers splayed across her lower back.

All that hard, male muscle against her belly and chest robbed her of speech and sent her pulse galloping. Breathless, she clung to him until the song ended, desire warring with common sense.

When the last notes died away, Jeremy stepped back, raised her hand to his lips, and brushed the barest whisper of a kiss across her knuckles. "Thank you, Carla."

No, thank you. Clamping her lips tight to keep from saying something stupid, she stepped back and blew out a shaky breath.

Back at their table, she yanked her gaze from the play of muscles beneath his shirt, climbed onto her barstool, and downed the rest of her drink.

Holy crap on a cracker, that was a close one. For a moment, she almost forgot her resolve to stay away from men until her head cleared. No way could she think straight with Jeremy so near. Time to put an end to this night.

She was reaching for her coat when the server stepped up and deposited something dark in a martini glass, along with another beer for Jeremy.

"Oh, we didn't order these—" Carla started.

"They're from your friend. She says to check your phone."

Carla sipped her third drink, something strong, fruity, and far too delicious, then checked her messages. "Motherfudge!"

Shari had slipped out with just a text. **SRY. This one is 2 cute. CYL.**

Jeremy sipped his beer. "Let me guess. They ditched us."

"I. Will. Kill. Her." She snatched a paper heart from the table and ripped it to confetti as she spoke. "She promised me no matchmaking."

"Well, technically..." He leaned onto his elbow and waggled his eyebrows. "Does leaving us alone really count?"

It totally counts. She forced her face to unfrown. "Sorry, Jeremy. I didn't mean to squash the mood. Guess I'm just too tired to enjoy myself." She took another sip. Why not? The drink was delicious, and it was as close to an apology as she'd get from her fickle friend. "Better not drive tonight." She tapped her phone to open the ride-sharing app.

His hand covered hers and gently squeezed. "It'll take forever to get a driver tonight. Let me give you a ride."

"But you've been drinking too." She eyed his glass. "You like ice in your beer?"

There it was again, his adorably sheepish grin. "Actually, it's ginger beer. I was supposed to be Leo's DD."

"Oh. Well, uh…"

He traced his fingertip over his sternum. "No funny business. Cross my heart."

Nibbling her lip, she deliberated. On the one hand, letting a guy know where she lived was stupid. On the other hand, he was right about the scarcity of drivers—and he'd only find out which building she lived in, not which apartment. She didn't have to let him come up, or even kiss him goodnight. Who said anything about kissing? Weird how her mind went there so quickly. Must be the alcohol.

"Okay, why not?" She unfurled her coat. "I mean, thanks."

As they left, the massive bouncer clucked his tongue. "You're gonna miss the piñata."

Jeremy linked his arm through Carla's. "I already won the best prize."

All the way to his car, her better angel yammered about the unwisdom of accepting a ride from a guy she just met, until he clicked his remote and the lights on a silver Tesla flared.

"This is me." He opened the passenger door and held it, waiting.

"I've always wanted to ride in one of these."

He flashed a cheeky smile. "In that case, I'll take the scenic route."

He did, too, steering north toward the stately brick halls of Puget Sound University. They cruised slowly through the historic homes of the Proctor District before turning onto the steep slope of North 30th Street. The port of Tacoma lay twinkling below, its lights reflected in the glassy waters of the Sound.

Carla wrenched her gaze from Jeremy's sharp-jawed profile and took in the scene. "Pretty, isn't it? In daylight it's just industrial ugliness, but at night, it's magical, like some fairy city."

At the stoplight, Jeremy turned to face her. "I have a good view of the port from my place. You should come by sometime."

"I'd like that." The words just slipped out, leaving her surprised and a touch embarrassed. Only a few hours ago, she'd disavowed everything connected to romance, dating, and men in general. Yet here she was feeling utterly relaxed while a strange man with a rumbly voice and a fancy car drove her God knows where.

The Tesla rolled silently, turning up the hill toward home. But Jeremy detoured again through the Stadium District, cruising slowly up a restaurant-lined stretch where bundled-up couples strolled under bare winter trees.

"Have you tried this place?" He pointed to the Art House Café.

"I haven't. Shari's been bugging me to sign up for one of those paint-and-drink nights they host." Not much of an artist herself, she'd love to have a go at capturing his profile—those dramatic dark brows, long, straight nose, sharp chin covered with salt and pepper scruff, and a full, bitable lower lip. His hair was trimmed close at the sides, but a longer top layer swooped over his brow as if artfully arranged there. Oh no, was he one of those guys who used a ton of product?

"Which street?" he asked.

Carla flushed. She'd been so busy studying Jeremy she'd lost track of where she was. Through the window, she spotted the elegant stone ladies flanking the entrance to Wright Park.

"A few more blocks. J Street."

He inclined his head, and a perfect wave of silver-tinged hair flopped onto his forehead. A graceful toss sent it back into place. *Like a stallion tossing his mane.*

Carla fanned herself. How long since she'd been with a man this devastating? Xavier was handsome enough, but over the last year their sexual connection had mellowed into something comfortable and—if she was totally honest—uninspiring. Like a quick, refreshing shower instead of a long, luxurious bath...with candlelight and rose petals...in a tub big enough for two...

"What are you thinking about, dream girl?"

"Oh, just work stuff," she lied. "Inventory, billing..."

He chuckled as he turned onto her street. "You must really love your job."

"Why do you say that?"

"Your expression. You look like a woman in love."

A fresh wave of heat washed over her. Good thing they'd almost reached her building. Another ten minutes in close proximity to Jeremy and her face would burst into flames.

"Up there. The Franklin." She pointed to the brick apartment block with cement griffins flanking the entrance. A memory tickled. "Say, isn't your last name Franklin?"

He nodded as he backed into a parking space.

"You're not my landlord, are you?"

Hard to tell in the dim illumination of the streetlight, but he seemed to be blushing. "The only building I own is my house."

He tapped a screen on the dashboard, and the car fell silent.

God help me. It had been so long since she'd been in this position—not even a first date, really, but a first encounter with a man she desperately wanted to see more of. She felt as tongue-tied as a teenager.

He reached for her hand. "Thanks for trusting me to take you home, Carla. It was truly a pleasure meeting you."

That's it? Just goodbye?

Dipping his chin, he gazed at her through thick, glossy lashes. "I'm a little rusty at this part, but I'd love to see you again."

Like an ingenue in a romance novel, she released the breath she didn't realize she'd been holding. "I'd like that. But I should warn you, I just got out of a relationship. I'm a little..."

"Raw?" His thumb stroked an arc over the back of her hand, the soft scrape of callus distractingly delicious.

"Skittish, I guess. I was planning to take some time off from the whole dating business, get my head on straight."

His smile took on a devilish tinge. "Your head looks perfectly straight to me. But no pressure. It's just—when heaven drops a treasure in your path, you shouldn't ignore it." He winced and chuckled. "I mean you. You're the treasure. In case that wasn't clear." He thunked his head back against the headrest. "Not exactly a poet, am I?"

She squeezed his hand. "What a lovely compliment. Thank you." She reached for his phone, resting in a compartment beneath the dashboard. "May I?"

He flicked the screen to life, and she entered her number. "Give me a call sometime."

On the sidewalk, a ruckus grabbed both their attention. A pair of street people shouted insults at each other. The woman clambered onto one of the griffins, removed her shoe, and hurled it at the guy below.

"Oh, Lord." Carla gave a weary sigh. "It's Aggie and Angel."

"Friends of yours?"

"Neighbors, on and off." She hooked a thumb over her shoulder. "There's a shelter up the hill. They like to hang out at the bus stop on the corner."

"Motherfucker," Aggie shrieked.

Jeremy's face settled into a glower. "I'll walk you to your door."

"No, you don't have to—"

But he was already outside, trotting around the car. He opened the passenger door and held it while she rose to her feet. His hand settled at the small of her back, his body close as she climbed the stairs—a shield against flying shoes, his warmth palpable even through her thick winter coat.

Note to self: thank Aggie tomorrow.

He followed her into the marble-tiled entryway, leaned on the closed door, and raked his fingers through his hair. "That was freaky."

She shrugged. "They're loud, but they've never hurt anyone as far as I know. Don't you get rowdy people down in Old Town?"

"Just when the Spar Tavern closes." The corner of his mouth quirked up as he reached for her hands. "Those old folks get pretty ripped at the Sunday blues concerts."

"Yeah, you gotta watch those oldsters." She grinned and let him tug her closer.

"Like me?" He stroked her arms, his touch firm and warm.

"Nah. You seem safe enough. And not very old."

"I'm ancient."

She raised an eyebrow and waited. *How old are you, silver fox?*

"Fifty-one."

Not so much older than her, and in phenomenal shape, by the look of him.

"And you, youngster?" His playful grin drooped. "Or am I not supposed to ask?"

"Forty-five."

He nodded. "A good age. Multiples of nine are lucky."

"Is that so?" She fiddled with the button of his pea coat. "What about prime numbers?"

He kneaded her arms gently, triggering a cascade of happy tingles. "Beautiful and smart. Very interesting, too. Guess it's my lucky night." He winced and ducked his head. "I can usually talk to women without sounding this cheesy."

"Lucky for you, I like cheese."

He threw his head back and laughed, a deep, throaty sound that made her insides tingle like champagne. Time to cut this off before she did something stupid, like inviting him upstairs.

"Well, I'd better go," she said with a sigh. "It's been a long day."

His gaze held hers. Neither moved.

Oh, what the hell. It's Valentine's Day.

"Thanks for a fun evening." Rising on her toes, she brushed her lips against his.

His grip on her elbows tightened. For a long moment, she hovered there, a sliver of air between them, his dark eyes locked on hers. And then he released a soft grunt, slid one hand up to cradle her nape, and kissed her breathless.

A rush of pleasure and need roared through her. His tongue stroked hers, a languid, hypnotic dance. Boneless, brainless, she pressed her breasts to his chest as her whole body and soul melted into a wanton puddle of *yes, yes, yes...*

Something hit the door behind them with a resounding thwack. "Cocksucking bastard!" Aggie bellowed.

Clutching her coat over her heart, Carla jolted backward, then yanked the door open. "Do you mind, Aggie? It's Valentine's Day, and you guys are ruining the mood."

The two combatants blinked at her. Then Angel dropped to one knee and folded his hands over his heart, gazing up at his sparring partner. "I don't wanna fight with you, baby. Let's go home."

"Well, since it's Valentine's Day." With a huff, Aggie slid down from the stone griffin, retrieved her shoes, and linked her arm with Angel's. "Happy Valentine's Day, pizza lady," she called out as they trotted back up the hill.

"Pizza lady? I thought you ran a vintage shop."

Laughing, Carla swiped a hand down her face. "Pizza place up the hill had a two-for-one special last month. I gave them my extra pie."

Jeremy squeezed her shoulder. "You're something else, Carla." He pecked her cheek. "I'll call you soon."

"Please do." Leaning on the door frame, she watched him drive away, then turned her gaze up to the stars, diamond-bright in the winter sky. "Wow. Thanks, Cupid."

Monday, February 15th

♥

The next morning, despite the hangover throbbing inside her skull, Carla grinned at her reflection as she brushed her fuzzy teeth. "I kissed a silver fox on Valentine's Day. Take that, Xavier."

She spit out a mouthful of foam. Foolish to kiss a guy she hardly knew, but so what? She'd probably never hear from him again.

Since Vintage Rapture was closed on Mondays, she enjoyed a leisurely start to her morning. Over coffee and a veggie omelet, she checked her phone messages. Nothing from Jeremy, but most guys stuck to the three-day rule before asking for a second date, right? Not that they'd had a first date, but still.

Shari had left a string of messages, though, ending with **CALL ME!**

"Okay, okay. I'll listen to you brag." Carla tapped the phone icon.

Her friend sounded breathless. "Oh my everlovin' God, what a night!"

"Good for you." She envied Shari's romantic bravado. Every new guy was *the one*, the best thing since sliced bread—until their connection ended. Then Shari gave a nonchalant shrug and moved on to the next tasty man. C'est la vie.

"...and he did this thing with his tongue. Ooo la la, the man is gifted!"

"I'm happy for you." She forked up more eggs. If she waited for Carla to finish squeeing, her breakfast would get cold. "Think you'll see him again?"

"He promised to call, but you know guys." Shari chuckled over the clatter of dishes.

Maybe she should take a page out of her bestie's book. "Shari, does stuff like this make you happy?"

"Mind-blowing sex?" She spluttered with laughter. "Hell yeah."

"Even if it's just a one-night stand?"

"Honey, sometimes a quick hookup is like a vitamin shot. Perks your ego right up. You should try it."

"I don't know." Carla nibbled her whole wheat toast. "That's never been my style. I prefer getting acquainted first."

"So ask him a lot of questions before you jump his bones. Speaking of tasty bones, how'd it go with your silver fox?"

Her face heated. "Oh, you know, just a goodnight kiss."

"A good one?"

"Excellent." Carla's phone pinged as a text notification appeared on the screen. Her pulse broke into a gallop. "Oh my God, Shar, he just texted. He's asking me to dinner on Friday."

"It's a sign," Shari squealed. "Say yes."

"What about the three-day rule?"

"Screw that. You like him, don't you?"

"Yeah, but—"

"Be brave, girlfriend! Some ego stroking from a hot silver fox is just what you need right now."

What if he wants to stroke more than my ego?

For the past twenty years, her love life followed the same predictable pattern: meet a guy, date for a week or two, fall into bed, fall into a routine, then cool off and break up. Her longest affair lasted five years, the shortest, six months. Maybe meeting Jeremy was a sign she shouldn't ignore. Time to break the chain, try something new. After all, the end of a casual fling wouldn't hurt as much, right?

"I'll do it." She gave her phone screen a loud smooch. "Thanks, Shar. You've inspired me."

Later that morning, ensconced in the quiet of her shop, Carla sorted decorations. For the run-up to Saint Patrick's Day, she'd move all the green merchandise to the front of the shop. She was sorting through garments for the window mannequins when a loud knock sounded. She automatically glanced at the front door, still securely covered with a metal grate and a Closed sign. No one there. Must be the door to the back alley. A delivery?

Dusting her hands on the seat of her jeans, she made her way back and peered through the peephole. Gary, her landlord, stood there rubbing his arms against the chill and talking to someone over his shoulder.

She opened the door and stepped aside to beckon him in. "Gary, hi. Long time no see."

"Carla, how are you?" He kissed both her cheeks before moving into the hallway, trailed by two taller, younger men with very familiar faces. *What the...?*

Leo's eyes widened as he glanced from Carla to a red-faced Jeremy. "Morning, Carla. This is your shop?" He bumped Jeremy's shoulder with his and whispered, "Did we know that?"

Holding Carla's startled gaze, Jeremy gave his head a sharp shake.

"You know each other?" Gary rubbed the back of his neck. "Well then, that makes it easier."

Carla's racing mind couldn't quite keep up. Normally, she'd be delighted to see Jeremy in her shop, but why on earth would he visit with her landlord? Unless...

Her stomach dropped as she recalled Jeremy's profession—commercial real estate.

Gary's jovial expression turned solemn. "Kiddo, I've got some bad news."

No! she screamed inwardly. *Please don't sell the building.*

Gary continued, his jowly face grave. "I'm afraid Linda's cancer is back."

Her chest hollowed. "Oh, no."

When she first leased this storefront, Gary's sweet wife had handed over the keys and walked her through the old building's quirks. Three months later, Linda's snowy hair was gone, her rosy cheeks pale and sunken from the ravages of chemo. But she battled back, and lately she'd glowed with robust health. The thought of her going through that ordeal again broke Carla's heart.

Gary swiped his watery eyes with the back of his hand. "Since our daughter moved to Chicago, it's just Linda and me managing all these buildings. Time to cash out so I can take care of my bride." He gestured to Jeremy and Leo. "These NTRC guys came along at the perfect time."

"NTRC?" she asked, her mind still reeling from the double whammy of bad news.

Jeremy's chin dropped to his chest. "North Tacoma Revitalization Consortium," he muttered.

Leo threw his friend a confused glance before adding, "We're investing pretty heavily in Sixth Avenue properties, and Mr. Park asked us to come take a look."

"Investing." She spit the word through clenched jaws. "Is that what you call it?"

Gary patted her shoulder. "I'm sorry, Carla. Truly I am. Maybe you can work out an agreement with the new owners." While Carla fumed, he led Jeremy and Leo through the shop, pointing out fixtures, electrical outlets, everything they'd need to transform her beloved, successful shop into yet another rubber-stamped chain store or overpriced eatery.

When Gary and Leo took their leave, Jeremy stayed behind. The sight of his crumpled expression and hunched posture stirred a twinge of sympathy in Carla's breast, but she squashed it down hard. With her livelihood on the line, she didn't have time to empathize with the sad rich guy, even if he was a phenomenal kisser.

Eyes downcast, he cleared his throat. "Carla, I swear, if I'd known—"

"What?" she snapped. "What could you possibly say to make this better?"

He took a halting step toward her. "When I realized this was your shop, I nearly lost my breakfast."

"Well," she said with a sniff, "that's a great comfort. I'm glad betraying me upsets your stomach." She stabbed a finger toward the front window. "There's a drugstore up the street. Maybe you can get an antacid. Or are you going to put them out of business too?"

Raising his palms, he backed away. "Look, maybe I can fix this. There are lots of properties for sale in the area. We don't have to buy this building."

Carla's rage fizzled to damp-eyed despair. "If you don't buy it, someone else will. Either way, my shop is toast."

"Carla." He reached for her hands.

She jerked away. "Don't. Should've known you were too good to be true."

Raking his hands into his silvery hair, Jeremy spun away and paced, muttering under his breath. His nausea must be catching, because her stomach roiled at the bitter irony of it all. Just a few hours ago, the memory of Jeremy's kiss filled her with giddy hope. Now, he'd extinguished not only that brief flicker of joy, but her entire livelihood. With Tacoma's rapidly rising rents, she'd never find another commercial space like this one. Hell, she'd probably have to move, leaving behind the apartment she loved.

Bile rose in her throat. "You lied to me last night."

He turned, his brow furrowed. "I swear, I didn't."

"Bullshit. You told me you didn't own my apartment building."

His shoulders drooped. "I don't, but the family firm does. It was my great-grandfather's first property in Tacoma." His mouth quirked in a wry smile. "We've been landlords ever since."

"Too bad you won't be mine."

"Maybe we could—"

"Cut the crap, Jeremy. We both know how gentrification works. You'll gut this place, slap on some glitter, and rent it out at twice the price to some snooty boutique locals can't afford to shop in." She pounded her fist on the glass counter, rattling the vintage jewelry inside. "Your ilk is sucking the soul out of Sixth Ave."

He held her burning gaze as he chewed on the plush lower lip she'd kissed last night. Then he gave a crisp nod. "Not this time."

"What?"

"You won't lose your lease. Vintage Rapture is staying right here. I give you my word."

She wanted to believe him, but his band of rapacious developers had devoured buildings throughout the neighborhood. How could one hot kiss break the cycle of destruction? Experience had taught her well—no matter how devoted a guy seemed in the early phases, love faded. Trust too. No kiss could ever be passionate enough to stop the march of greed.

His jaw muscles bunched in an annoyingly sexy way as he stepped closer. "Are we still on for Friday?" When she didn't answer, his eyebrows flicked up. "Please?"

Indecision churned in her belly. She didn't trust him—how could she? And yet, his promise was her only hope of keeping the shop.

She sucked in a deep breath. "Okay. I'm probably going to regret this, but I'll give you a chance."

The smile he gave her was so dazzling it was simply unfair. He squeezed her hands. "You won't regret it. I'm going to make this right. You'll see."

Friday, February 19th

♥

"Look." Jeremy leaned over their table to be heard over the clatter of silverware and laughter from the surrounding tables. "I know it hurts to see a favorite shop close, but the NTRC has brought new life to a lot of old buildings, most of them vacant. New businesses on Sixth Ave means more jobs, and more customers for existing businesses like yours. You've got to look at the big picture."

"The big profit, you mean." Carla gazed through the wall of glass at the moonlight-spangled Puget Sound below. "Gotta keep those investors happy. Who cares about merchants who get displaced?" She felt the tiniest twinge of guilt over grilling him like this. Friday night reservations at Harbor View were hard to come by, and the grilled halibut and prawns they'd feasted on were damned expensive. But it would take more than seafood and pretty promises to win her trust, especially from the guy whose firm was trying to gobble up her building.

She'd kept her temper in check through cocktails, starters, and the main course by avoiding the touchy subject at hand. But after a lemon drop martini and half a bottle of excellent Columbia Valley Sauvignon Blanc, her tact was slipping. "All your talk of economic life cycles is damned cold comfort when you throw me out on my ass, and my perfect store location becomes another stupid hipster brew pub."

Jeremy's nostrils flared on a deep inhale. "I promised you I'll do whatever it takes to keep your shop safe. It won't be easy. Franklin Development isn't the only player in the NTRC. But you're right—there's a difference between renovating a vacant property and displacing a thriving business."

"Damn straight there is." She glared at him—hard to do effectively with candlelight dancing in his dark eyes.

With an upward quirk of his lush lips, he raised his dessert fork and his eyebrows.

She slid her half-finished slice of marionberry pie toward him, then forked up a morsel of his white chocolate and Rainier cherry cake.

Jeremy took a bite of pie, closed his eyes, and released a groan that echoed between her thighs. Why did he have to be so distractingly gorgeous? Hard to hang onto her anger when he licked his fork, each languid slide of his pink tongue washing her core in a fresh wave of heat.

His grin widened. "Wow. Phenomenal."

Amen. She stabbed a cherry from atop his cake, swirled it in the white chocolate buttercream, and popped it into her mouth. His irises darkened as he followed the movement. She'd like to order a tub of this decadent frosting and spread it across his...

She gave her head a sharp shake. *Eyes on the prize*—Vintage Rapture, not the hot, tasty man watching her lick her lips.

"Jeremy, you really think you can keep the wolves from my door?"

He nodded slowly, his gaze never leaving her face. "I always keep my promises."

"I'll hold you to it." Not that she could do anything about it if he turned out to be like all the other guys who'd let her down. Which was most of them. Okay, all of them.

"Hey." His warm, heavy hand closed over hers. "Can we talk about something else?"

"Sure." All this verbal jousting was ruining her appetite—a shame, with two delicious desserts to share. "Let's see—where did you go to school?"

"PLU for undergrad, U Dub for my MBA."

She arched an eyebrow, surprised he'd chosen the University of Washington instead of some Ivy League college back East. "How about high school?"

"Stadium. You?"

"Same." She couldn't help grinning. "Too bad. If you were one year younger, I'd have met you back then." She forked up another bite of pie. "I bet you were a jock."

His rumbling laugh crinkled the corners of his eyes. "You'd lose that bet. I was a band nerd."

"You?" Hard to imagine a young Jeremy without his chiseled physique. "Must've been the best-looking band nerd in school."

He chuffed a laugh. "Why, thank you. Wrong again, though. I was skinny with zits and a cheesy wannabe mustache."

Impossible to imagine this powerful, poised, handsome man as the awkward boy he described.

His lips quirked as he caught her ogling his firm physique.

Blushing, she lowered her gaze to her plate. "What did you play?"

"Saxophone and piano. Sang in the choir too."

"Seems a long leap from music to real estate."

He rubbed the bridge of his nose. "Yeah, well, family business. How about you?" He licked a bit of cherry goo off his plump lower lip. "Let me guess. You were a theater geek."

"Not fair. You know I'm into costuming."

"I'll bet you were the star of every show."

She shook her head. "Strictly backstage. I was costume mistress. I still love finding the perfect outfit to reflect someone's personality. You can't do that with off-the-rack contemporary stuff. That's why I built my business around vintage clothing."

"Did you study fashion in college?"

"Psychology, actually." She scooped up the last bite of pie.

He arched an eyebrow. "Intimidating."

"How so?"

"Hard to hide my motivation from you." A devilish smile bloomed across his face, revealing a deep dimple in his right cheek—a dimple she'd like to explore with the tip of her tongue.

He straightened and signaled the server. "Could I interest you in a coffee before we say goodnight?"

"Where?"

"At my place." He pointed toward the steep hills of Tacoma's Old Town neighborhood. "I'm right nearby, and I bought a new espresso machine yesterday. After a minor steamed milk eruption, I've learned to make a passable cappuccino."

She really, really wanted to take him up on his offer, and to peek inside a real estate developer's luxury home. He probably had magnificent views of the Sound. She imagined standing beside him, mug in hand, drinking in the view— the glittering bay, and the broad shoulders straining his tailored shirt, and his tight, toned butt, and...

As if reading her mind, he leaned in and lowered his voice to a teasing, velvet tone. "I've got a great view. And a baby grand."

"You're going to serenade me?"

"If that's what it takes to keep you by my side a little longer."

She'd probably regret this tomorrow. On the other hand, indulging their mutual attraction might motivate him to save her shop from the vultures. That thought left her feeling a bit slimy, but her business was on the line.

All's fair in love and war, right?

Heart thrumming, she pushed back her chair. "Okay. One coffee."

The view stole Carla's breath.

Flickering flames from the gas fireplace reflected in the wall of windows overlooking the Puget Sound. While Jeremy fiddled with his hissing espresso machine, she took in the sweeping panorama that stretched from Gig Harbor to the port, transformed by darkness to a twinkling fairyland.

"How do you get anything done?" she asked with a sigh. "If I lived here, I'd spend all day watching the boats go by."

"Sometimes, I do." He appeared at her elbow, holding a steaming mug. "Decaf, extra foam."

She sipped. "Not bad."

"Worked at Starbucks all through college," he admitted with a crooked smile.

"A man of many talents." She wiped milk from her lip. "I was promised entertainment as well."

"Ah, yes." He interlaced his fingers and stretched his hands, palms out. "Have a seat and I'll tickle the ivories for you." His playful grin suggested he'd rather be tickling other things. No doubt he'd be damn good at it, what with those strong, nimble fingers.

Hiding her grin behind her cup, she curled up on a squashy leather armchair. He sat at his gleaming Steinway, the muscles of his broad back shifting beneath his crisp dress shirt as he rolled his shoulders.

"Hmm, what should I play?" He rested his fingers lightly on the keys. "Does the lady like classics, or something more modern?" He teased liquid notes from the instrument—soft at first, like a merry brook trickling over rocks. Then the music deepened, filling the room from gleaming parquet floor to peaked ceiling.

Eyes closed, Jeremy swayed, caressing the piano like a lover. His silvery hair flopped over his brow as he rocked forward, and then his lips parted and he began to sing in a deep, rich baritone—each word a caress as he sang of love and longing, moonlight and mystery, fate and forever.

Chills chased down her spine as she drank in the unconscious grace of his movements and imagined those agile fingers dancing over her bare skin.

Her body swayed in time with his as the music unfurled. When he reached the final notes, she released a low moan.

As if awakening from a trance, he blinked and straightened. "That bad?"

"That good." She hated to admit it, because wanting him this desperately threw her off guard. Tonight was only supposed to be a bit of flirtatious fun, a balm to her bruised self-esteem. But now, caressed by his velvet voice, she perched on the edge of her seat, yearning for him to stroke so much more than her ego.

Right on cue, the clouds parted and a pearly full moon cast its glow on Jeremy's thick, silvery hair. He slid over on the bench and extended his arm. "Come. Help me pick out another song."

Helpless to resist, she sat beside him. She fought to focus on the book of Broadway tunes he flipped through, distracted by the warm length of his thigh pressed against hers.

"This one." She touched his wrist. How could a mere wrist feel so enticing? Just a bunch of little bones and sinew, covered with satin skin and a whisper of dark hairs... She cleared her throat. "I worked on a production of this musical in college."

"Whew, that's a high one. I'll have to transpose down. Let's see—" He pressed the keys, sang a note, shook his head, and moved further down the keyboard. Finally satisfied, he launched into a soaring love ballad. His shoulder nudged hers again and again as he reached for the high notes, and by the time he belted out "*And oh, the glorious feeling*," her heart was fluttering like a hummingbird and her panties were soaked.

As the swoony love song came to an end, he leaned in so close his breath lifted her hair and sang softly into her ear, "*The lane where you live*...J Street and North Fifth." He chuckled. "My favorite spot in the whole city. Even if your neighbors interrupted our goodnight kiss."

His gaze dropped to her lips, but he made no move to come nearer. The choice was hers. The last bricks in her wall of reserve crumbled and fell away. Keenly aware of the crackling tension between them, she leaned closer and murmured, "There's no one interrupting us now."

His thick lashes lowered as he whispered her name, and then his lips pressed to hers, soft and warm and so delicious she thought she'd melt right off his piano bench. This was a man she could trust with her pleasure, an artist who would tease her to a blazing crescendo.

His arm slid around her waist, snugging her against his muscled chest. With a low groan, he teased her lips apart and licked into her mouth. With a whimper, she raked her fingers into the silver silk of his hair.

"Carla." He broke away, his eyes dark and sharp with need. "Will you stay with me tonight?"

Too lust-stunned to speak, she clutched him tighter.

Hot, wet kisses trailed down her throat. "Please, angel. Let me love you. I want to feel you coming on my tongue, then on my cock."

His words kindled an anticipation so keen she couldn't hold back a helpless moan. His hand slid to her breast, kneading softly through her silk blouse. When his thumb brushed her nipple, electric sparks of bliss drew a whispered "Yes, yes, yes" from her lips.

He rose from the bench, pulled her into his arms, and walked her backward to the sofa, where he eased her onto the cool leather cushions.

"You're so beautiful." His callused fingertips skimmed her jaw.

And she felt beautiful, lying beneath him as his bright, dark eyes drank her in from head to hip. Xavier had never gazed at her with such intense focus. It was heady stuff, stronger than the wine that loosened her tongue and her inhibitions.

This is madness, her last remaining brain cells squawked. *He's not going to spare your shop just because you fuck him.*

But if she held back, if she wrapped herself in icy reserve and left them both pulsing with frustration, she'd still be vulnerable. If she surrendered to mutual desire, at least she'd have the memory of this beautiful night to sustain her during the battle to come. And perhaps an intimate knowledge of her opponent.

Heart hammering, she closed her eyes and shoved her worries into a dusty corner. *He wants me. I want him.*

Time to get out of her head and enjoy this moment of serendipity.

She slid her arms around his neck and pulled him down atop her. His weight pushed her deeper into the cushions as his questing tongue plundered her mouth. Greedy for more, she undulated beneath him, arching her breasts against his solid heat until he broke the kiss to nip at her collarbone and unbutton her blouse. The roughness of his fingers against her sensitive skin brought her nipples to stiff peaks.

He put those dexterous fingers to good use, quickly freeing her from her lace bra. She lay topless, arms flung overhead, flushed with arousal. Hunger twisted his elegant features into something rough and feral. But he held back, only skating his fingertips over the outer curve of her breasts. Impatient and desperate for more, she whispered, "Please."

Her silver fox lowered his head and swept his tongue over her tender skin, drawing ever-tightening circles until his lips closed over her nipple. When he sucked it deep into the heat of his mouth, a zing of pleasure shot straight to her clit.

His free hand kneaded her other breast as he teased first one tight bud, then the other. Wracked by exquisite torture, she felt the warning flush between her thighs. If he suckled her much longer, she was going to come—and he hadn't even touched her pussy. How was this possible?

His hand slid down to dip inside her waistband. Her breath caught when he released her nipple and trailed kisses down her belly. Lifting her hips, she helped him slide the tight pants down her legs.

He rose onto his knees and raked her bare body with his burning gaze. "You are stunning."

Hard-won experience had taught her not to fall for flattery, but his words sparked a giddy buzz in her chest. Their embrace had left him adorably rumpled—hair mussed, once-crisp shirt now untucked and wrinkled by her grasping hands, and a glorious erection tenting his wool slacks.

"Why are you wearing so much clothing?" she teased. "Not fair."

With a rough grunt, he grasped the hem of his shirt and yanked it over his head. Buttons skittered over the hardwood floor.

Kneeling before him on the couch, she ran her greedy hands over smooth muscle and dark chest hair that tickled her palms. Masculine, powerful, sleek. She kissed his jaw, relishing the faint scrape of scruff against her lips, then pressed an open-mouthed kiss to the crook of his neck.

"Carla." She loved the sound of her name on his lips—but what she loved even more was his hungry groan when she rocked her pelvis against his hard, heated shaft.

Gripping her shoulders, he pressed her back onto the couch, the leather cool against her feverish skin. Firelight flickered in his dark eyes as he skimmed down, down, taking her panties with him, then rising again to caress her inner thighs as his worshipful gaze zeroed in on her pussy.

"So beautiful," he murmured, stroking her slick folds with his thumbs. "Like an orchid, flushed and open for me."

His touch had her arching off the cushion, reaching for more. With a grunt, he gripped the outside of each thigh and buried his face between them. She gasped, delighted to find his tongue just as talented as his fingers. Long, languid licks brought her closer and closer to bliss, until she trembled on the precipice, ready to fall.

"Please, Jeremy," she begged, writhing in his grip.

With a devilish chuckle, he flicked his tongue over her clit and slid two fingers inside her. Her nerve endings sang as he nipped and licked and sucked. Within moments, her grip on his hair tightened. Her breath stuttered, held, then burst forth in a ragged cry as overwhelming pleasure ripped her apart.

When the room rematerialized and she could see again, there he was, kneeling between her thighs, his mouth flushed and slick with her arousal. With a feral, foxy grin, he wiped his lips and pulled her to her feet. "Bed."

Giddy and boneless, she let him tug her down a hallway to a bedroom that shared the same harbor view. Not that she gave a damn about watching ships glide into port now. She only had eyes for Jeremy. Graceful as a panther, he lowered her to the mattress, then unfastened his belt and let his slacks fall to the floor. Moonlight threw the planes and angles of his muscular body into sharp relief, like some magnificent marble statue. He slid off his boxer briefs, then toed off his socks and crawled over her, his thick erection bobbing.

Her hand closed over velvety skin and stony hardness. She stroked him from root to plush crown and moaned when he thrust into her grip. With a primal growl, she lightly scratched her nails over his plump pink balls.

Shuddering, he squeezed his eyes shut. "Carla, I need to be inside you."

She lay back, still clutching his cock.

"I'm, uh, gonna need this." Chuckling, he pulled free from her greedy grasp and reached for the nightstand drawer. Her mouth watered as she watched him roll a condom over his rigid shaft. Settling between her parted thighs, he leaned in to kiss her deeply. The blunt head of his cock nudged her opening once, twice, then he filled her in one exquisite thrust.

"OhGodohGodohGod," she gasped, stretched tight, every nerve ending sparking like fireworks.

For a long moment he just held her, muscles tense, his breath hot at her temple. And then, with a low, hungry moan, he began to move.

Lifting her legs to grip his hips, she met him thrust for thrust, delirious with bliss. He rode her fast and hard, sweet words tumbling from his lips as his body tightened in her arms. He ravaged her mouth with a fierce, deep kiss, then growled against her bruised lips, "Come for me, angel." Thrusting deep, he ground his pelvis against her clit. "Let me feel you coming on my cock."

One hard thrust, another, and she was flying, impossible pleasure singing through her veins. She buried her cries in the crook of his neck. His cock pulsed inside her as he rode his own release.

Panting, slick with sweat, she slowly drifted back to earth. Jeremy collapsed half atop her, boneless and heavy. Their frantic coupling had pulled the sheets loose, and they lay in a snarl of damp cloth. He kissed her shoulder, then gifted her a heart-melting, blissed-out grin. "That was...you are...wow."

"Amen." Her giddy laughter dislodged his softening cock.

He rolled from the bed, trotted to the bathroom to deal with the condom, and returned with a glass of water and a fluffy towel.

"My queen." He helped her sit and, while she sipped, blotted the slickness between her thighs.

Still giggling, she set the glass aside and snuggled among the pillows. "I haven't felt this good in years."

"Neither have I, lovely one." The mattress dipped as lay beside her and covered them both with a fluffy duvet. "I'm so grateful I found you."

A faint warning light flashed somewhere in her rattled brain. Sure, Jeremy was an amazing man, but she'd be smart to keep her expectations in check. Nothing real could happen between them until the danger to her shop was past.

She should go now, before she sank too deep into her feelings. Just collect her clothes, thank him for a wonderful evening, and jet. Plenty of time to sort things out later.

But before she could summon the will to leave, he enfolded her in his strong arms, snugged her against his warm, heavy body, and peppered her face with kisses. "Stay with me, Carla."

"I can't."

"You can. Just a little longer." His fingertips traced hypnotic whorls over her skin, lulling her toward sleep.

"Just a few minutes," she murmured. Closing her eyes, she surrendered to his magical touch.

Saturday, February 20th

♥

The scent of coffee invaded her cozy dream of tinkling piano notes, soft caresses, low moans...

Curtains swooshed open. Bright sunlight stabbed through her closed lids. Clutching the covers to her chest, she bolted upright in bed—*Jeremy's bed*.

And there he stood, his lips curved in a devilish smile, his silver hair gleaming in the morning sunlight. Dressed already in workout pants and a snug black T-shirt, he looked so delectable it was unfair.

"I made you a little breakfast." He set a tray on the bedside table, then sat beside her, resting his hand on the rumpled covers over her thigh. "I hated to wake you, but you said you had to get to your shop early."

Carla raked her fingers into her sex-snarled hair. She hadn't meant to spend the night. This was supposed to be a onetime indulgence, not a breakfast-in-bed kind of deal. But here sat Jeremy, his hand on her knee, his gaze soft and fond. And "a little breakfast" turned out to be fluffy scrambled eggs, a croissant, a dish of jam, and fresh fruit, along with an artfully swirled cappuccino. She couldn't just bolt after he'd gone to so much trouble.

She offered a weak smile. "Aren't you eating?"

"After my run." He flashed a flirty grin. "I'd ask you to join me, but I doubt you could keep up in those sexy boots." He gestured to an armchair by the window that held her neatly folded clothes.

She sipped the heavenly coffee he pressed into her hands. "What time is it?"

"Almost eight."

She nearly spewed coffee across his bedcovers. She never slept so late, not even on her days off. And today definitely was not one of them. "Oh Lord, I have to go."

"You should eat at least a few bites." Sliding his hand beneath the covers, he stroked her from knee to ankle and back. "We expended a lot of energy last night." Up and down, he traced a tingling path. "Any chance for a repeat performance?"

She nearly choked on a mouthful of eggs.

His warm smile drooped. "Okay," he murmured, his voice flat. "I'll leave you be. Maybe I'll see you around sometime." Rising stiffly, he gave her one last longing glance before disappearing into the hallway.

"Jeremy, wait!" Pushing the tray aside, she threw back the covers and dashed after him. "I didn't mean goodbye, I'm just—"

He stood frozen by the front door, one running shoe on, the other in his hand. Watching through narrowed eyes, he waited.

"Arrgh." She scrubbed her hands down her face, searching for words to unsnarl her tangled thoughts and feelings. "This was more than I expected. Last night was—" She released a helpless sigh. "Phenomenal, actually, and I would like to see you again."

"Yeah?" The corner of his mouth twitched upward.

"Yeah. And thank you—for breakfast, and dinner, and the music, and..." She drank him in from head to toe, every gorgeous, unexpected inch of him. "All of it."

Biting his lip, he slid closer and took hold of her hips, his grip light as his thumbs traced arcs on her bare skin.

Oops. In her rush to catch him before he left, she'd neglected to pull on clothing, which explained the erection straining his workout pants.

She crossed her arms over her breasts, a pointless gesture. With a chuckle, he peeled off his T-shirt and handed it over. "Here. You'll catch a chill."

She pulled the soft, warm cotton over her head and hoped he didn't see her inhale his bourbon and leather scent.

"Thanks." She shuffled her bare feet on the cool tiles. "So, uh, I really do have to get to work. Saturday is my busiest day, and my assistant is out of town for a wedding."

"Sounds like you could use a hand."

She blinked rapidly. "You want to help in my shop?"

"I want to get to know you. What better way than spending time in the business you're so passionate about?" His eyes darkened as he traced her jawline with his forefinger. "I like you when you're passionate. I'll meet you there at...?" He cocked an eyebrow.

This is absolute crazy sauce. But the words popped out unbidden. "I open at ten."

"Right." He pulled a workout jacket from the brass coat tree and zipped it over his beautiful bare chest. With a chuckle, he glanced down at his crotch. "Down, Junior. Now is not the time." He cupped Carla's cheek. "Just pull the door shut when you go. See you soon, gorgeous."

Jeremy proved a quick study. A half hour after arriving with coffee and pastries, he was sorting garments like a pro. Carla rang up a handful of vintage concert pins for a pair of giggling teens, then looked up to find the shop empty of customers.

He held up a tuxedo jacket with satin lapels. "This is small enough to fit you. Put it in the women's section?"

She peaked at the faded neck tag. "Hang it with the men's eveningwear. Women will shop in the men's section, but few men will give the women's section a glance."

"How much?" he asked, lifting the tagging gun.

She checked the seams. "The lining's worn but intact. Twenty-five."

He plucked a price tag from the tray and fastened it to the sleeve. "Wish my job was this simple."

"Guess you can't just stick a price tag on a building, eh?" She smooched his temple, doing her best to ignore the twinge of anxiety tightening her jaw.

"Hey." He captured her hand and spun her to face him. "We'll figure this out, okay? I have a meeting with the NTRC directors on Monday."

Despite his reassurance, she couldn't help but worry. His clear dark eyes held no hint of deception, but everyone had an angle. What was Jeremy's?

He sat on the rolling stool she used for stocking lower shelves, then pulled her onto his lap. Giggling, she snuggled into the circle of his arms.

He rested his chin on her shoulder. "I like this place. It reflects you."

"How so?"

"It's colorful. Sparkly. Full of surprises. Everything in here has an interesting story."

She fanned herself with her hand. "Why sir, are you trying to turn my head?"

"And remove your pants." He nipped at the sensitive crook of her neck.

Carla let herself sink into the sweetness of the moment and imagine a future where this fleeting connection could actually mean something—where Jeremy would be a regular visitor to her shop, and her bed. Where they'd watch the sun rise and set through his glorious panorama window, or from her tiny balcony. Where...

The doorway bell jingled as Shari sailed in. "Oh, my stars and garters." Her sparkly fingertips fluttered to her heart. "Carla-bean, you didn't tell me you had company today."

Jeremy tipped an imaginary hat. "Delightful to see you again, Miss Shari."

Carla sprang to her feet. "Jeremy was just helping me with some new inventory."

"Uh huh," Shari deadpanned.

"Because her assistant's out of town," he added brightly.

"Right." Shari's lips twitched in a "gotcha" grin. "Just make sure you lock the door before you two start rumpling the merchandise."

Carla flushed hotter than a teakettle. "Nobody is rumpling anything in my shop."

The entry bell jingled again, and Jeremy's friend Leo strode in, looking crisp and ready for business in a starched blue dress shirt and creased khakis. "Red alert, Jer. Your dad's on the warpath."

"Shit, shit, shit." Jeremy pinched the bridge of his nose. "Better head him off." With a huge sigh, he grasped Carla's shoulders and pressed a soft kiss to her lips. "Sorry, angel. I have to go. Call you later?"

She nodded, trying to ignore the nibble of worry in her gut.

"You coming?" Jeremy asked his friend on his way out.

"Be right there." With a lustful grin, Leo slid closer to Shari and grasped her hips.

But Shari was having none of it. She poked Leo's chest. "What the hell was that about?"

His broad shoulders slumped, and he shot Carla a guilty glance. "The old man is pissed because Jeremy's thwarting a juicy deal with Carla's landlord. After we lost out on buying Bangers Tavern, Jer's dad put him in charge of acquisitions on Sixth Ave. Kind of a test for when he takes over the family firm. Jer's in a tough spot. He loves the old pirate, but it's just not in his nature to be as ruthless as Walter Franklin."

Carla clutched a feathered cocktail hat to her chest, a totally inadequate shield for the plundering to come. Her voice tightened to a raspy whisper. "He promised he wouldn't let them sell my shop."

Leo's gaze shifted from her to Shari and back. "I'm afraid that might not be possible."

Eyes blazing, Shari gave his shoulder a thwack. "Then you better get your ass out of here and go help him."

Ducking his head, he complied.

Shari rushed to Carla and hugged her tight. "Oh, darlin'. Any idiot can see Jeremy's in love with you. He'll move the moon and stars to save Vintage Rapture. I'm sure of it."

Carla pushed her friend away. "In love with me? We just met a week ago."

"I recognize the signs. Moony eyes. Goofy smile. Helping in your shop, for goodness' sake."

Carla's heart wanted to believe it, wanted to trust the feeling growing between them. But her brain pushed back ruthlessly. How could one hot night together be enough to make him stand up against his family, especially with profit on the line? Her shop was doomed—and so was her romance with Jeremy.

Don't give up on me, angel.

Jeremy's text came close to midnight. More than twelve hours had passed since he took his leave from Vintage Rapture with a hurried kiss and a promise. More than twelve hours of worry, self-recrimination, and worst-case scenarios, each more catastrophic than the last.

Sitting up in bed, a tablet propped on her knees, she'd been searching commercial real estate listings from Seattle to Olympia—a masochistic exercise in exposure therapy. If she gave herself time to get used to the idea of moving somewhere else, when the bad news came, she'd be prepared. If that was even possible.

Round and round her thoughts spun like some out-of-control carnival ride—all the years she'd spent building Vintage Rapture. It had taken two years of running in the red before she finally turned a profit. By the time she could afford to pay herself a decent salary, her credit was strained and her savings almost gone. The Sixth Avenue location was a blessing, but a temporary one. She couldn't ask her landlord to hang onto the building when he needed the money to care for his ailing wife. And she couldn't expect Jeremy to defy his family for a woman he'd just met. She was well and truly screwed.

She started and erased her reply to Jeremy a dozen times. Finally, she typed **I'm sure you're doing your best** and hit the Send key.

Should she ask him to call? No, he'd hear the hurt in her voice and make more promises. Better to keep her distance. Not that she'd get any sleep tonight, but at least she could rest her bleary eyes.

Another text bubble appeared on her screen. **Can we talk? I'm outside.**

Holy crap on a cracker.

Her traitorous heart pounded as she glanced out the bedroom window. Stars twinkled in a crystalline sky, their light fragmented by ice blossoms on the pane. He must be freezing out there. But if she let him in, they'd end up in her bed. How could she think clearly pressed up against his naked body? The wound inflicted by Leo's news this morning had barely begun to close. She couldn't let Jeremy rip it open again.

On the other hand, if he'd come to see her at this ridiculous hour, he must have news.

Her thumbs shook as she typed **On my way.**

Pulse thundering, she brushed her bed-mussed hair and pulled on thick workout pants and a ski sweater. The landing outside her apartment was silent, but TV voices blared from her neighbors' apartment across the hall. She pushed the button and jiggled with nervous energy while the ancient elevator grumbled its way up to the fourth floor. She was about to give up and take the stairs when the elaborate metal grate finally opened.

Downstairs, she spotted Jeremy's shadowy outline through the frosted glass. With a deep, shaky breath, she opened the door.

Her mental armor slipped at the sight of him. Wrapped up in a puffy ski jacket, thick wool beanie, and a fuzzy scarf wound up to his nose, he looked like a kid heading out to play in the snow. But when he tugged his scarf down, the streetlights' harsh glare deepened the lines framing his tightly pinched lips.

He tugged his knit cap off and scrubbed a hand through his mussed hair. "Can I come in?"

She threw a panicked glance over her shoulder. She couldn't very well ask him to stay out here in the icy cold, but if she brought him up to her apartment, the gravity of her warm bed would pull them in.

"Just the entry, then?" He twisted his scarf in his gloved hands.

"Sure. Of course." With a weak smile, she beckoned him inside and took a seat on a bench opposite the mailboxes. Pale light from the streetlamps shone through the glass bricks at her back, casting long shadows on the marble floor.

Jeremy sat beside her, leaving a cushion of space between them. He pulled off his gloves and folded them in his lap. "So, I guess Leo told you."

"That your dad was pissed, yeah." She gave a dry chuckle. "Sounds like something a teenager would say to her boyfriend."

His answering laugh rang hollow and brittle. "It does. Unfortunately, he's also my boss. And at almost eighty, well—changing his mind isn't exactly a strength."

"Family businesses can be fraught, right?"

"Very." He laid his hand palm up on the bench and raised his eyebrow, a silent plea.

She nestled her hand into his. If this was the end, she wanted one more sweet touch to remember him by.

"From my father's point of view, I'm betraying the family. Leo sees my side of things. My sister too. But the others—" He tipped his head back against the glass bricks. "They're all about the bottom line. And your building is a juicy prize."

"Well then." She fought the tremor in her voice. "Good thing I've been scouting new locations."

Jeremy knit his brows. "Carla, no. You love that location."

"You said it yourself—businesses come and go. It's all part of a neighborhood's life cycle."

He pinned her with a stern gaze. "I'm not giving up yet. Not by a long shot. On Monday, I'll convince the NTRC to keep your business where it is."

"How? Aren't they all about the bottom line too? Or do they actually care about the community?"

"They talk a good game, but..." With a sigh, he raked his fingers into his moon-silvered hair. "I swear, I'll find a way."

"Why, Jeremy?"

He blinked in confusion. "Why what?"

A wave of tenderness for this would-be white knight pulled the words from her tight throat. "Why go to all this trouble for me? You're gorgeous, talented, rich, an amazing lover. You could have any woman you want."

He grasped her arms and pressed his forehead to hers. "Because you're the one I want, and even if I never get to hold you again, I can't live with myself if I have a part in destroying your business." He held her gaze for a breathless moment, and then he kissed her, long and warm and sweet.

It took every bit of strength Carla had to gently push him back. "I adore you, Jeremy. And I want you so much—but I just can't."

He closed his eyes, and his lips thinned to a slash. "Okay. I understand." He slowly pushed to his feet. "I won't forget you, Carla." Shoulders slumped, head down, he shuffled to the door and out into the wintery night.

A sob tore through her. It was so unfair! After so many lackluster relationships, the one guy who made her heart sing was the one she couldn't have. She could have fallen in love with him so easily. Hell, she probably already had, but what was the point? His firm's real estate grab poisoned their love before it ever got off the ground.

She swiped away her useless tears and rode back upstairs alone.

Monday, February 22nd

♥

"Hold still. You're gonna make me cut your ear."

Carla gave up trying to look her friend in the eye and faced the big mirror, where she watched Shari snip and fluff and fuss.

When she finally called her bestie and spilled the sad unraveling of her almost-romance, Shari insisted on some therapeutic pampering in her salon.

Shari set down her scissors and shook a squeeze bottle of dye. "These highlights will bring out the gold flecks in your eyes."

"More like the red in my eyes."

Shari massaged Carla's shoulders like a trainer pep-talking a battered boxer. "Fate makes mistakes sometimes. She'll send another guy your way before you know it."

"Fate's a sadistic bitch." Carla glowered at her reflection. "Why send me the perfect guy and then destroy our chance at happiness?"

"Some things are beyond our understanding," Shari intoned, squirting dye into a plastic basin. "All you can do is learn from the situation and move on."

"I haven't learned shit," Carla grumbled, "except maybe..."

Shari raised her perfectly groomed eyebrows and waited.

Carla twisted in her seat again. "Shar, was I a fool for breaking it off with him? I mean, he wants to be with me despite all this mess. Maybe I could've used that to save my shop."

"Then why did you break it off?"

She slumped beneath her protective cape. "I couldn't live with myself if I used him that way. He's a good man. It's not his fault he's stuck in this awful position, any more than it's my fault or the landlord's. Gary's wife has cancer. What's he supposed to do? We're all stuck."

Shari gave a sage nod. "Sounds like Jeremy's risking a lot for you."

"How would you know?"

"Leo cancelled our date yesterday to help him prepare a fancy presentation for his development group." She gripped Carla's jaw and forced her head forward again, then patted her cheek. "Takes a special kind of love to voluntarily make PowerPoint slides."

Carla snorted. "Love? We just met a week ago."

"But that's where you were headed."

"Maybe." *Probably. That's why this hurts so much.* She narrowed her eyes at Shari's reflection. "Did you bend Leo's arm?"

"Absolutely not." Shari crossed her heart.

In the purse at her feet, Carla's phone tootled. Shari scooped up the bag and dumped it in Carla's lap. "Answer it."

"Probably just some robocaller."

"Cursing out robocallers is therapeutic. Answer it."

With a sigh, Carla dug out her phone, then nearly dropped it when she spotted Jeremy's number on the screen.

"Carla, hi. How are you?" His voice sounded flat, defeated.

"Sad. Worried too, but mostly sad." Her burst of honesty astonished her. She was usually better at putting on a brave front.

"Damn. I wish I had better news."

"Oh God." Her voice hitched. "My shop's toast, isn't it? How long do I have to move out?"

"Easy now." His chuckle was a pale shadow of the deep rumbling laugh that warmed her down to her toes a few days ago. "I still have one more trick up my sleeve."

Part of her wished he'd just cut the cord binding them together. Why give her hope only to smash it on the jagged rocks of reality over and over?

He continued, in a tone so crisp she could see the sharp jut of his jaw, the fire in his dark eyes. "I'm going to fix this, Carla, even if you won't see me again. I hope you will, but this is a stand I should've taken long ago." His tone softened. "When I have news, I'll be in touch."

"Okay. Thank you." But he'd already hung up.

Shari eyed her in the mirror, a smug smirk all over her perfectly made-up face. "Told you. That man isn't ready to let you go. You better buckle in and enjoy the ride."

Sunday, February 28th

♥

"I am absolutely not going to sing!" Carla gulped the last of her drink and glared at Shari, seated across from her at one of Bangers Tavern's high-top tables—the same table where they'd met Jeremy and Leo two weeks ago. With no holiday on tap, Bangers was back to its usual Sunday night karaoke.

"You don't have to sing, for Chrissakes." Shari nabbed the last tater tot from the plate they were sharing. "Want another drink?" She held up her empty glass and searched the crowd for a server.

"Several."

Why not? Tomorrow was her day off, and enough fruity cocktails might help her forget the misery of the past week—no more calls from Jeremy, no leads on a new location, and business was sagging in the downtime between Valentine's and Saint Patrick's Day. Add four steady days of sleet and slush, and Carla's spirit was thoroughly squashed.

"Hi, ladies. What can I get you?" The server twiddled the end of her long pigtail and grinned around a mouthful of gum.

Carla tapped her empty glass. "Another of the pink special, please."

"One Pink Señorita. And you, ma'am?" She looked at Shari.

"Another Green Demon, please."

The server bopped away, bouncing in time with the 90s boy-band anthem a trio of bearded guys were murdering on stage.

Carla shuddered. "Ma'am. Ugh."

Shari elbowed her. "Lighten up, sunshine. That girl is twenty-two at the most. To her, we are ma'ams. So what?" She rolled her shoulders and gave her ample boobs a shake. "We're a couple of hot cougars on the prowl." After fluffing her hair, now strawberry blonde, she patted Carla's into place. "Those highlights suit you. Let me take them lighter next time?"

"I swear, I'll look like a zebra by the time you're done with me."

"A very sexy zebra. Rrraowrr."

Carla swatted Shari's hands away. "That's not what zebras sound like."

"She's right," a deep voice rumbled behind them. "It's more of a giggling sound, like a donkey on laughing gas."

"Leo!" Shari hopped from her barstool and threw her arms around his neck.

Funny, Shari hadn't mentioned Leo once this week, always changing the subject whenever Carla asked. She figured their fling must've run its course. But here he was, burying his fuzzy beard in the crook of Shari's neck. Their easy affection was like salt rubbed into Carla's shredded heart.

"Hi, Leo." Carla flashed him a phony smile, then linked her arm through Shari's. "Would you excuse us for just a minute?" She tugged Shari to the hallway by the restrooms. "I didn't know we were expecting company."

Shari's grin was just as false, a sure sign she was up to something. "Don't be silly. Leo's fun. You could use some laughs to pull you out of this silly funk."

Silly funk? Shari's flippant comment stung. Carla straightened her spine. "You know what? I'm feeling a little flu-ish.

Why don't you and Leo share my drink? I'm gonna head home."

"You'll do no such thing. Come on." Shari towed her into the restroom, where she fussed with Carla's blouse, opening an extra button. "There. Now put this on." She held out a tube of lip gloss.

"For Chrissake, Shar. You think anything can be fixed with the right shade of lipstick."

"Fixed, no. Improved, yes."

When they were both primped to Shari's satisfaction, Carla let herself be towed back to their table. "Just one more drink, then I really have to go."

Leo's jovial smile broadened. "You can't leave just yet. You'll spoil the surprise."

Shari smacked his arm and gave him a bug-eyed stare.

"Surprise?" Carla scowled. "What are you two up to?" She fixed Shari with a glare. "I told you, I'm not singing."

Up on stage, Dawn, the bar's owner, took the mic. "How y'all doing tonight?"

The crowd clapped and hooted.

"Next up, we have a very special song for a very special lady. Give it up for Jeremy."

Carla gripped the table's edge to keep from toppling off her stool. She poked Shari's arm hard. "Why didn't you warn me?"

"He asked me not to. Now shut up and let the man serenade you."

When Jeremy stepped onto the stage, Leo waved and hollered, "She's over here, bro."

"Great," she muttered. The man she couldn't have was going to try and sing his way back into her bed—like some cheesy rom-com. And in the morning, he'd break her heart again.

Cheeks flaming, she slumped on her stool. *I'm not strong enough for this.*

Jeremy conferred with the old guy running the karaoke machine, then pinned Carla with a gaze brighter than any spotlight. "This is for you, angel."

The music swelled, and he began to sing.

All conversation stilled as Jeremy crooned an old jazz classic, sweet words of music, the moon, and finding heaven in his lover's arms. Every poignant image washed through her like warm surf, champagne fizz, shooting stars—she didn't have words to describe this intoxicating feeling.

But Jeremy did, and he sang them all to her. Brimming with love and longing, his hypnotic gaze left her powerless to look away.

His voice soared and dipped, a warm, velvet tone that wrapped so tight around her heart she couldn't breathe.

Carla bit her lip hard, but it was no use. A tear trickled down her cheek. He was tearing her apart, and she could only sit there defenseless as he poured out his song of hope and love—sweet, pointless words that shredded her.

When his performance ended to thunderous applause, Jeremy hopped down and made his way to their table, his progress delayed by backslaps and praise. Carla rose from her stool, poised to flee, but Shari's hands clamped onto her shoulders and forced her back down.

Despite his warm smile, tension flickered across Jeremy's face as he closed the distance. He accepted Leo's hug and the peck Shari gave his cheek, then whispered something to his friend.

Leo grinned broadly. "C'mon, Shari. Let me buy you a drink."

"She has a drink," Carla volunteered, but they were already slipping into the crowd.

Jeremy sat beside her and flashed a heart-twisting, lopsided grin. "So."

"So." She fiddled with the stem of her glass, fighting the urge to chug its contents. "You said you'd contact me when you had news."

"I did." His eyes sparkled under the Seahawks blue and green twinkle lights. "And here it is." From his pocket, he pulled an envelope embossed with the name of a legal firm.

She stared at it, then at him.

"Open it."

With trembling fingers, she tore the envelope and removed a multi-page document bearing an official-looking seal. She flipped through, skimming the dense legalese.

"What is this? An eviction?"

He chuckled. "I asked Leo to go easy on the jargon, but he said we need all these clauses." His warm, heavy hand closed over hers. "It's your new lease."

"New?"

"The building has changed hands."

Her stomach tightened. "Who bought it?"

He waggled his fingers. "Say hi to your new landlord."

Words stuck in her throat. She gulped downed her drink, shook off the harsh burn, and croaked, "Are you out of your mind?"

His gaze darted from the paper to her incredulous scowl. "It was the only way."

"Jeremy, I can't date my landlord." She crumpled the contract it in her sweaty fist. "This would always be hanging between us."

His words tumbled fast. "No, see, that's the beauty of it. Your rent is frozen for five years." He pried the document from her hand, flipped to the third page, and tapped the final paragraph. "Once you sign, I can't raise it, no matter what happens. Your shop is safe."

"For five years?"

He lifted her hand to his lips and pressed a kiss to her knuckles. "I figure that's long enough to know whether what we have will stick. If it doesn't work out between us, we'll renegotiate the lease."

She gulped her drink to quench her suddenly parched throat. "You're bribing me to be your girlfriend?"

"No, I—shit." He winced. "I swear, I didn't mean it that way. I wanted to just give you the building, but Leo says that would be a tax nightmare, and—" Planting his feet on the rungs of his barstool, he rose and waved. "Damn it, Leo, get back here."

She grasped his arm and pulled him back down. "Hang on. Let me catch my breath."

He sat, his eyes searching her face while she tried to wrap her buzzing brain around this bombshell he'd just dropped in her lap. Really, it was a very generous offer. Jeremy couldn't single-handedly stop the march of gentrification, but he was putting his own capital on the line to give her a five-year reprieve. If she signed, she could keep her shop whether or not she dated him. Talk about your leap of faith...

Finally, when her pulse slowed from a blur to a mere gallop, she squeezed Jeremy's hand. "I don't know what to say."

His handsome face solemn, he laced his fingers through hers. "Whatever you decide, I want to thank you."

"For what?"

"For being the catalyst I needed. Franklin Developments doesn't reflect my values—a fact I've ignored for too long. I'm striking out on my own." He pulled a business card from his pocket. "J. Franklin Property Management. No more predatory real estate deals. I want to help grow businesses, not shut them down."

"Jeremy!" She gripped his hand tight. "I can't let you do that for me."

"I'm doing it for me, angel. For my own peace of mind." He kissed the inside of her wrist, shooting distracting shivers right to her core. "For the first time in ages, I feel good about my work. And I have you to thank. You inspired me, Carla."

An almost unbearably sweet, fluttery feeling filled her chest and nearly lifted her from her chair. With tears prickled her eyes, she whispered, "That's the loveliest thing anyone's ever said to me."

While the next singer belted a schmalzy country ballad, Carla held Jeremy's hand and gazed into his beautiful dark eyes. Even with the sports-themed decorations, rowdy karaoke crowd, and greasy bar food, she couldn't imagine a more romantic setting—and she couldn't imagine sharing it with any man but Jeremy.

The gruff old graybeard who'd manned the Cupid shooting gallery on Valentine's Day shuffled to their table and off-loaded a tray of goodies: tater tots topped with Monterey Jack cheese, buffalo chicken strips, green onions, and a spicy ranch dressing, along with a split of champagne.

"Did you order this?" She asked Jeremy.

The old guy grunted. "On the house. Dawn's a real softie, eh?" He hooked a thumb over his shoulder. "Something about this place brings couples together. Dawn thinks it's the carved cupid above the bar." He waggled his grizzled eyebrows. "I think it's the tots."

Carla thanked him, then grabbed his elbow before he could walk away. "Say, um—" She glanced back at Jeremy's dimpled, swoony smile. "Any chance we could get these to go?"

Carla followed Jeremy's Tesla back to her apartment building, where they found a rusted-out van blocking the garage entrance. Music blared from inside the old junker, along with raucous laugher. She rolled down her window as Jeremy hopped out of his Tesla and knocked on the van's passenger window. The door opened, and when the skunk-scented smoke cleared, Carla spotted the grinning faces of Aggie and Angel.

She waved to her noisy neighbors. "Hey, Aggie. Nice wheels."

"Ain't she beautiful?" Aggie beamed. "We got a kitchen and everything. Me and my Angel are gonna hit the open road."

Jeremy cleared his throat. "Any chance you guys could move your van? *My* angel is tired, and I need to put her to bed."

"I bet you do." Aggie and Angel exchanged a look, then collapsed in hysterical laughter. Angel finally sat up. "Trouble is, we're outta gas money."

Rolling his eyes, Jeremy pulled a twenty from his wallet.

Angel snapped a salute. "Thanks, man. You take good care of Pizza Lady, ya hear?"

"Oh, I intend to."

Obstruction removed, they parked and entered the building. The moment the elevator doors slid closed, Jeremy pressed Carla to the wall and feathered kisses along her jaw, then down the leaping pulse in her throat. Her desire unfurled to the rhythm of his swirling tongue.

With a giddy giggle, she unwound her scarf to invite further exploration. "The neighbors will be scandalized."

"Good thing you're dating the landlord," he murmured between burning kisses.

"Hey." She smacked his shoulder. "I thought you didn't own this building."

"It's complicated." His devilish grin tempted her to bite his succulent lower lip.

The ancient elevator finally grumbled to a halt on the fourth floor, and they spilled out into the hallway, nearly upending a dusty potted palm.

"Well then." She dug her key out and opened her apartment door. "You want to inspect the property?"

"The only thing I want to inspect is you. In detail." Once inside, he pressed her against the closed door and peppered her face with kisses as he peeled off first his coat, then hers, letting both drop where they stood. "Bedroom?"

"This way."

Kissing and groping, they stumbled across the living room and collided with the sofa. Something tumbled to the floor. Carla couldn't bring herself to care—every atom of her body was focused on getting closer to Jeremy. Blood hummed in her veins so loudly she was sure the whole building could hear.

When she finally bonked into the mattress, she threw herself backwards and pulled him down atop her and relaxed into his embrace. Well, almost.

"What is it, angel? You're tense." His brow creased as he rose onto his elbows. "You don't want this?"

"I do." Sliding her hands into his silky hair, she searched his face. "But I'm afraid to trust this feeling."

He rolled off her and nestled to her side, his head propped on his hand. "I understand. It's been a wild ride. We just met two weeks ago, and already you've turned my life upside down." His hand crept beneath her blouse and traced hypnotic arcs over her fevered skin.

She brushed her thumb over his cheekbone. "It's scary to feel this much so soon."

His slow, soft smile glowed. "I don't trust my luck either, but all signs point to this being an excellent idea."

"You think so?"

"I'm betting on a positive return on my investment." He nuzzled her neck, sending a ripple of pleasure down her spine to pool between her thighs.

"Who could resist all this dirty talk?" Giggling, she unbuttoned his shirt and toyed with the dusting of coarse, dark hair beneath. "You seductive devil."

He rested his forehead against hers. "My work has taught me to recognize a once-in-a-lifetime opportunity. And Carla, this is it." He kissed her, slow and deep, exploring and claiming. When he dragged his mouth from hers, his voice held a rough edge. "I won't pressure you or hurry you, but please know I am one hundred percent sure about us. And I'm sticking around until you tell me to go away."

The gentle persuasion of his kiss lulled her doubts as she opened to him. He nipped her lower lip, then soothed it with his velvet tongue.

Shifting his weight, he pressed her into the pillows, melting her bones and making her skin so sensitive, every touch sparked delicious shivers. In the pale light of her bedside lamp, his bare torso gleamed like sculpted marble. And when he stripped her clothes away and drank her in with his fevered gaze, she felt just as beautiful. He caressed her with his fingertips, and all thought surrendered to sensation—hot, firm body above, cool, crisp sheets below, and urgent need pulsing between her thighs.

Rising from the bed, Jeremy quickly shed his own clothing and dug a condom from his pocket. He stretched out beside her again and, with a hungry groan, kissed her deeply while his clever fingers parted her folds and stroked until she trembled and begged.

She wrapped her hand around his rigid shaft. "Please, I need you inside me."

Grasping her hips, he rolled onto his back and positioned her to straddle him. Wicked delight sparkled in his dark eyes as he handed her the foil packet. She ripped it open and rolled the thin sheath over him. At her touch, his breath caught.

Later, she promised herself, she'd explore every inch of him with her fingers and tongue. She'd suck his beautiful cock until he cried for mercy. But right now, her need was too urgent. Lifting onto her knees, she positioned his plush crown at her entrance and, holding his glittering gaze, sank down until he filled her completely—so hard, so hot, so deliriously good. Slowly she rose, then glided down again.

Jeremy let her set the pace, his gaze never leaving her face as pleasure undid them both. When she sped her motions, he pinched and rolled her nipple, the shadow of pain sharpening her bliss. Arching her back, she stretched out her hand to stroke his silky balls. His eyes shut tight. His breath stuttered.

Tightening his grasp on her hips, he forced her to ride him faster. "Come with me, Carla," he growled. "Show me how to get you there."

She guided his thumb to where she ached for his touch. "Yes," she moaned. "Faster."

He rubbed her tingling clit in tight circles as he fucked her in swift, shallow thrusts. The surrounding room narrowed and blurred until all she could see was Jeremy gasping and straining beneath her. Bliss surged through her, wave after pulsing, brilliant wave. Curling forward, he buried his face between her breasts and growled her name as his cock throbbed with his own release.

Blissfully spent, she fell forward, her sweat-slicked body pressed to Jeremy's while his fingertips traced delicious circles over her back and hips.

His chuckle rumbled. "What do you think, angel? Worth the risk?"

She sighed against his neck, a whoosh of utter contentment. "Absolutely."

Saint Patrick's Day

♥

Six o'clock at last. Carla rang up her final customer, then flipped the door sign from Open to Closed.

While the metal grate lowered with a metallic grumble, Jeremy wound his arms around her waist. "Good day, angel?"

"Excellent." She tipped her head back to rest against his shoulder. "I doubt there's one green item left in the shop."

"Gotta hand it to you. I never associated Saint Paddy's Day with glamorous vintage clothing, but you made it work."

"What can I say? I'm a marketing genius." She turned into his embrace and planted a lingering smooch on his lips.

"You are." He smiled into the kiss. "But there is one more green item left." He pulled a slim box from his hip pocket.

"Jeremy?" Blinking rapidly, she gazed from his face to the gift and back.

"Open it." He held her hips loosely while she unknotted the green satin ribbon. Inside, a tiny shamrock with emerald leaves and a diamond center hung from a whisper-thin gold chain.

"Jer, it's...I'm...wow." Tears stung her eyes.

"Turn around." He deftly fastened the necklace, then pressed a kiss to her nape.

She gazed into the mirror on the counter, delighted by how perfectly the delicate charm nestled in the hollow at the base of her throat. "It's so beautiful. No one's ever bought me a Saint Patrick's gift before." Throwing her arms around his neck, she peppered his face with kisses. "Thank you."

"Well, it seemed only fair after all the luck you've brought me. The record shop up the street signed on for a partnership, and it's looking good for the tea and spice place too." He nuzzled her temple. "Sure you're not Irish?"

She chuckled into the crook of his neck. "With a name like Portofino?"

He looped his arms around the small of her back and tugged her tight against him. "Well, they say everyone's Irish on Saint Patrick's Day. Think they'll have green beer at Bangers?"

"I bet they will. And some kind of green sauce on the tots."

He waggled his eyebrows, a sexy gleam in his eye. "Mmm, tots. Let's go."

Thanks for reading! I hope you enjoyed Carla and Jeremy's steamy little love story as much as I enjoyed writing it.

Hungry for more? Check out the ***Bangers Tavern Romance*** series set in Tacoma, Washington's favorite neighborhood bar. Each book in the ***Bangers Tavern Romance Series*** features a different holiday celebration, starting with ***Christmas Rekindled***.

When two Scrooges collide under the mistletoe, their kiss blazes too hot to handle.

Stuck with her cranky, injured dad over the holidays, all Charlie wants for Christmas is a break. A temporary job at

Bangers Tavern is the perfect way to let off steam and escape Dad's criticism. But why does the hunky bartender hate her on sight?

River's holiday wish: avoid his matchmaking mother, ride out his grief, and flee the holiday fuss. Bangers Tavern is his refuge until sassy, snarky Charlie sashays in, just as smoking hot as when they first met. And she doesn't even remember him. Ouch.

A fake date or two should get their interfering families off their backs. No big deal, right? But shared holiday celebrations stir up messy feelings and irresistible desire. When greedy developers come gunning for the bar they both love, River and Charlie must team up to save it.

Come to Bangers Tavern for an enemies to lovers tale of reconciliation, found family, holiday shenanigans, and the steamiest Christmas miracle ever.

"I loved this story. Charlie and River have amazing chemistry with both of them having their own baggage. The Christmas vibes gave me all the feels. A perfect escapism. I especially appreciated how Charlie is part Lebanese as it gives snippets of a different culture. A feel good holiday romance where the love scenes were quite spectacular."

—Liv Arnold

Order *Christmas Rekindled*

Read on for a sample of ***Christmas Rekindled***, as well as info on the rest of Sadira Stone's steamy, swoony, laugh-out-loud romance books—and cocktail recipes from Bangers Tavern!

Christmas Rekindled Chapter One

♥

"Hey, what's a guy gotta do to get a beer in here?" Dad bellowed from the living room.

Charlie Khoury crumpled forward and thunked her head on the kitchen table. Between her dad's demands and the cheesy Christmas music blaring on TV, she was never going to finish this website redesign.

"Most wonderful time of the year, my ass," she grumbled as she nabbed a can of Rainier from the fridge and a tin of Pringles from the cabinet. Maybe that'd keep him happy and quiet long enough to complete her project.

Who'da thunk she would miss her cramped apartment in Portland? Sure, her roommates were slobs, but they fetched their own food and respected a closed door. Closed doors meant work in progress. Closed doors were sacred.

Not to Dad. He'd keep hollering until she emerged from whatever corner she'd squirreled herself into. And thanks to his ancient router, the kitchen was the only room with a decent Wi-Fi signal.

She found him on his lumpy recliner, a Sudoku magazine on his lap, watching a Christmas special. Only the first of December, and already the holiday music was inescapable.

Setting his refreshments on his TV tray, she surveyed his stained bathrobe and bare, hairy legs, the right one encased in a plaster cast. When had he stopped taking care of his appearance? True to his Lebanese roots, Dad was usually a snazzy dresser. Tonight, he looked like he'd been dragged through a bush. Backward.

She rested her fists on her hips. "Doc says you're supposed to get up every hour, Dad. You don't want to get a blood clot."

He didn't even look up from his puzzle. "Doc says to elevate my leg. So I'm elevating it." He wiggled his toes and reached for the beer. "Thanks, doll."

"Sure." She patted his shoulder. As much as this enforced proximity was a pain in the ass for her, it must be worse for Dad. He was a mover, a shaker—ask him and he'd tell you so himself. At length. But a stoned driver crunched Dad's delivery van, landing him on disability for at least two months. With his shattered tibia and bruised ribs, he was going to need help until January when he got his walking boot. So here she was—home for the holidays.

Joy, joy, joy.

She trudged to the kitchen and poured herself another cup of coffee. At least here in Dad's house she wasn't battered with constant reminders of Marvin, who'd abruptly moved out just before Thanksgiving. Turned out he'd been carrying a torch for his college girlfriend back East—his newly-single, no-longer-ex-girlfriend. That news hit like a bolt out of the blue. As far as she knew, she and Marvin were fine, then wham! They weren't in love, not really, but they'd been comfortable for three years, her longest romantic relationship ever. The sex was great, they shared lots of laughs, and she figured eventually...

She thought they were all set. She thought her life was all set. And now, she found herself questioning everything.

The front door rattled, then banged open. Anna strode through, wearing pastel scrubs beneath her puffy parka, arms loaded with shopping bags. She set them at her feet, swiped a hank of hair back from her forehead, and hitched her scowl to one side. "Pringles, Dad? Honestly?"

Holding his youngest daughter's gaze, Dad ripped the foil from the can and stuffed a stack of chips into his mouth. "Mmm." He waggled his thick black eyebrows as he crunched.

Anna strode over and snatched the beer. "No alcohol while you're still on pain meds. And wipe those crumbs off your mustache. Looks like a dirty whisk broom."

"You're a real Scrooge, you know that?" Dad wiggled his butt, settling further into his seat, grabbed the remote, and flipped to a boisterous sports report.

Shoulda known he wasn't supposed to drink. Shrugging off a twinge of guilt,Charlie hefted two shopping bags and headed for the kitchen. Anna followed with the rest.

"So, still no luck on getting him a home health aide?"

"Nope." Her sister's reply crackled with irritation. "His insurance won't cover that, not for broken bones."

Charlie grumbled under her breath, "I'm gonna break more bones if he doesn't stop bitching."

Anna spun, wielding a bunch of celery like a sword. "Don't you dare, Charlie. He's our father, and it's effin' Christmas. Christmas is about family, remember? We can't leave him alone to fend for himself." She poked Charlie's sternum. "About damn time you showed up to do your fair share."

Charlie splayed her hands. "I'm just—being cooped up together is so freakin' frustrating for both of us. And my work—"

"Which you can do anywhere." Anna slammed a can of pineapple on the counter. "Some of us can't work from home. Some of us—"

"I know, squirt." Charlie stepped behind her sister and squeezed her shoulders. "You're a far better daughter than I am."

Anna growled and kept unpacking.

"I'm not being snarky. You're a freakin' saint, coming over to check on him every day. You must understand how frustrating it is, spending all day cramped by these four walls and Dad's opinions. About my looks, my clothes, my hair, my love life, my work." She loaded sliced turkey and cheese into the fridge. "He never picked on you the way he did—does—on me."

Anna sank into a chair and massaged her temples. "He would if he knew how much I want to leave my husband. But I haven't told Dad because I don't need his B.S. on top of Brandon's. Especially not during the holidays." She fixed Charlie with a sharp glare. "Were you even gonna visit this Christmas? I mean, if Dad hadn't got hurt?"

Charlie's shoulders sagged. "Honestly, I was going skiing on Mount Bachelor if I could scrape together the cash. Guess that makes me a shitty daughter."

Anna patted her hand. "Well, you're here now. Back in your twin bed, just like in the good old days."

She snorted. "Old, maybe, but not good. Not since Mom—"

Anna tensed. "It is what it is, right? Why don't you go stretch your legs? I'll watch TV with Dad. Maybe we'll set up the Christmas tree."

"Oh God, does he still have that tacky old thing?" When they were little, Charlie and Anna would sit cross-legged beside the shiny aluminum tree while Mom read Christmas picture books aloud. Their ancient color wheel lamp grumbled as it rotated, illuminating the tinsel branches in blue, red, green, and yellow. After Mom died, Aunt Hala and Uncle Fred helped them pick out a real tree each year.

But last Christmas, out of the blue, Dad resurrected the tinsel tree, along with those tacky ornaments—Styrofoam balls wrapped in shiny red thread. Alone in the living room at midnight, Charlie unhooked one, rubbed its satiny surface against her cheek, and wept.

After stowing the groceries, she went back to the guest room, still furnished with matching twin beds. Someone, probably Aunt Hala, had updated the décor with new linens, throw pillows, and decorative knickknacks. But if you knew where to look, you could still spot the faint outline of long-gone posters she and Anna clipped from fan magazines.

Charlie bundled up in her leather bomber jacket, knit scarf, and beanie, enough to keep her warm on the short walk to her favorite hometown bar. The happy noise of Bangers Tavern would help her shake off this itchy claustrophobia.

Hands stuffed in her pockets, breath puffing like a locomotive, she rounded the corner onto Sixth Avenue, Tacoma's sixteen-block stretch of night spots, vintage clothing boutiques, record shops, restaurants, and cannabis dispensaries. The yeasty, sugary scent wafting from Legendary Doughnuts almost lured her in, but she craved a different treat: a fat, juicy, grease-dripping-down-your-elbows burger topped with crispy fried onions and melty cheese curds, with a side order of the crunchiest, golden-est tater tots this side of the Cascades, washed down with a Mac & Jack's African Amber.

Hopefully, Dawn would be working tonight. How long since she last saw her former boss and surrogate mom—one year? Two? Charlie's cheeks heated with shame.

She stepped around a grizzled old guy shouting slurred curses at an invisible foe, demurred when another wild-eyed guy offered her some "choice Indica bud," and gave a wide berth to the boisterous dude-bros smoking outside Jazzknuckles. Fairy lights and glitter snowflakes twinkled from the wedding gown resale boutique, and a plastic Santa holding a fat joint grinned from a record shop's window. She grinned back at him. The businesses on the Ave might change, but the funky vibe stayed the same. Even on a Tuesday night, this stretch was packed with fun seekers, street people, and college kids from nearby Puget Sound University, her alma mater.

Her smile widened when she reached Bangers and inhaled the tempting odor of greasy bar snacks. The bouncer was new, big as a mountain, with a shaved head and a sweet baby face. He checked her ID, then motioned her through.

She stopped in the doorway and let the familiar sights, sounds, and smells transport her back to her college years, when she spent most nights here schlepping beers and burgers. Same wooden bar, dents and cigarette burns preserved under a layer of shiny varnish. Same neon beer signs, same beer coasters and beer ads covering the walls, same TVs broadcasting a hodgepodge of sports. Not that anyone was paying attention. Nothing had changed. After all, why mess with perfection?

Same noisy, eclectic crowd, too—snarky old farts hunched over their beers at the bar, frat boys with popped collars, sharp-eyed pool sharks. Way in back, rowdy dart players hooted over good scores and bad ones. Gum-chomping servers wove through the throng, trays held high, keeping customers well-watered.

Charlie inhaled deeply and grinned. *Good to be home.*

She plunged into the crowd, jabbing with her elbows when needed. At five foot two, she was easy to overlook—but only once. Damned if she was gonna let some bulky behemoth step on her toes. "Coming through. Watch yourself, Bubba." She skirted guffawing college kids in PSU Lumberjack hoodies and climbed onto a barstool.

The lone bartender's long braids flew as she spun from the taps to the counter and back, moved with amazing speed, but Charlie knew from years of experience it'd be awhile before she got something to quench her thirst. The place was slammed.

A woman wearing a Seattle Mariners ballcap atop short gray curls emerged from swinging doors behind the bar, patted the petite bartender's shoulder, and started filling beer glasses. She'd chopped off her dreadlocks and grown a little wider across the seat, but there was no mistaking that mischievous grin, those tawny, freckle-dusted cheeks.

Charlie felt her heart swell in her chest. Dawn was still here.

From the barstool at the end of the bar, a gruff geezer hollered, "A man could die of thirst in this joint." Another familiar face. *What's his name again?*

"Keep your pants on." Dawn turned, foam-topped beer in hand, and froze. Her plump face lit up like Christmas. "Charlie?"

The thirsty customer grumbled, and Dawn slammed his beer in front of him, sloshing a quarter of its contents onto the bar. "Shut yer yap, Gus. Don't you recognize our old friend?"

Gus squinted at her, then at Dawn. With a shrug, he slurped his beer.

The boss leaned her elbows on the counter. "Too pickled to remember much. Been coming here for twenty years, and last week he called me Donna." She pinched Charlie's cheek. "Good to see you, angel. Thought you were living in Portland now. What brings you back?"

"Dad broke his leg on the job. Nasty crash. My sister watches him nights, and I've got the day shift."

Without asking, Dawn handed Charlie a Mac and Jack's, her favorite. "Still doing that computer stuff?"

"Web design and maintenance. It's portable, so—" She shrugged and sipped her beer. "Say, do you still serve that burger with the fried onion rings?"

"Sure thing, doll. We're slammed though, so it'll take a while." Dawn snatched a packet of pork rinds from a rack behind the bar. "This'll keep you alive. I'll tell Diego to put a rush on it."

"Diego's still here?" She tore open the packet and stuffed a handful of crunchy, porky delight into her mouth.

"Best fry cook on the Ave. I'm lucky he hasn't moved on to one of those fancy new places," Dawn said over her shoulder as she pulled more beers. "It's not easy to keep good people. And now Cassie, my head server, is back in Minnesota for the holidays. Her mama's sick. Might be her last Christmas, so I couldn't say no."

An idea tickled the back of Charlie's brain. Hardly any of her college friends lived in Tacoma anymore, and these past few days cooped up with Dad had her itching for some lively company. If she could rake in tips like she used to, she'd easily earn enough to go skiing in January. "How long will she be gone?"

"Cassie? Till January." Dawn's sharp brown eyes narrowed. "Why?"

All her best decisions in life had been made quickly, a matter of trusting her gut. And right now, her gut-o-meter buzzed and flashed like a slot machine. She pasted on a confident grin. "Because I'm stuck here caring for Dad for at least that long. Might as well earn a few bucks on the side. You know I can handle the job. What do you say?"

"Well, now." Dawn slapped her towel onto the bar and grinned. "Looks like my Christmas wish has been granted." A bell behind her dinged, and a brimming plate appeared on the pass-through window. She set it in front of Charlie. "On the house. When can you start?"

"Soon as I finish this." She lifted the burger, a real jaw-stretcher, and took a bite of cheesy, beefy, crisp-onion, fluffy-bun heaven. Diego's special sauce oozed out the other side and dripped onto her tots.

"I'll get the paperwork." As she headed toward her office in back, Dawn nudged the bartender. "Kiara, say hi to Charlie. She's gonna step in for Cassie."

Kiara flashed a bright smile. "Howdy, Charlie. Is it Charlene?"

"Charlotte." She popped a tot into her mouth. Just as crispy as she remembered. "I'd shake your hand, but—" She waved her greasy fingers. "You all alone back there?"

The bartender rolled her eyes. "River's late. Again. If he weren't so charming, Dawn woulda canned his ass long ago."

"Oho, charming, am I?" A deep baritone voice at her elbow spun Charlie around, but the guy had already slid behind the bar. Tall. Blond. Broad shoulders beneath a crisp black shirt. Lean but muscular, more like a dancer than a football player. His hair flopped into his eyes as he bent to scrub his hands. His short golden beard framed plush lips. Mismatched earrings: a small oval onyx on the left, a silver anchor on the right. Thick brown lashes.

Blue eyes, I'll bet. Breath held, Charlie waited.

Greenish hazel with flecks of amber. His gaze flicked up and pinned hers for a moment that seemed to stretch on and on. Then those bright eyes scanned her from top to bottom. One eyebrow flicked up as his lips spread in a devilish smile. "Hello, new girl."

Happy little fireflies danced in her stomach. Words stuck in her throat.

"Not so new." Dawn smacked a stack of papers onto the bar.

Totally focused on pretty boy's dazzling smile, Charlie hadn't seen the boss's approach. She took the pen Dawn proffered, cleared her throat, and began scribbling her contact information.

"Charlie used to work here, about—what was it, hon'?"

"I, uh—started in '09, I think. And I left in '14."

In an instant, River's expression shuttered—brows lowered, eyes narrowed, lips clamped in a tight, straight line. He picked up a bar towel, flung it over his shoulder, and silently turned to the beer taps.

Dawn scowled and elbowed him. "Don't be rude, River. Say hello to Charlie. She's taking over for Cassie."

"Hello, Charlie." His voice dripped icicles.

Kiara hip-bumped him. "Be nice, Riv. Who pissed in your Cheerios?"

Without further comment, he moved to the far end of the bar where a gaggle of college-age girls awaited refreshment. When he greeted them, they erupted in giggles. His high wattage smile reappeared as he muddled mint and cucumber in tall glasses, his forearm muscles flexing below rolled-up sleeves.

Kiara leaned on the bar and sighed. "Real lady killer, that one. Earns more in tips than the rest of us combined."

"I feel sorry for his girlfriend." Charlie tilted her head toward the too-pretty jerk.

"Oh, he doesn't—"

"Enough gossip." Dawn shooed Kiara away, then leaned closer. "Sorry, kiddo. River's usually such a charmer. I'll have a word with him."

"No worries, boss. I don't need to join his fan club to work here." She tilted her chin toward the end of the bar where River whipped out drinks with impressive speed and flair. "And I'll give him a run for his money on those tips."

"You always had the golden touch with customers. Still taking those belly dance classes?"

"Yeah, down in Portland." There's another thing she'd miss—she was supposed to dance her first solo at her troupe's holiday party. All that practice for nothing.

Once Charlie finished her dinner and application forms, Dawn introduced her to the rest of the staff: Eddie Volkov, the wiry barback, Jojo Williams, the bouncer; Lana Lopez and Rosie Chu, the harried servers.

"Thank God and little baby Jesus." Rosie tossed her electric blue curls. "Can you take the back section?" She waved toward the pool tables and dart boards. "That's usually Cassie's. They're feisty tonight. And thirsty."

Charlie glanced down at her feet, glad she'd chosen flat ankle boots instead of heels. She rolled her head and shoulders like a boxer warming up. "Bring it."

Dawn patted her shoulder. "That's my girl. C'mon, I'll get you a tray and an apron."

She followed Dawn to her little office in back and collected her supplies: a POS terminal for credit card payments, and a shallow apron with pockets for her cash caddy and pens. She tied the apron around her waist, popped a stick of cinnamon gum into her mouth to cover her burger breath, and sashayed into the mob.

Funny how, after six years away, it all came back to her, so easy and comfortable: balancing her tray overhead while sliding through the crowd like an otter through kelp, the sassy grin and friendly banter that filled her apron pockets with tips. A month of this and she'd have enough spare funds to join her housemates' ski trip to Mount Hood.And maybe, if she spent her evenings away from Dad, she'd have her sanity, too.

****

Six hours later, Dawn clanged the ship's bell above the bar. "Closing time. Drink up, folks." She twirled the dial on the sound system, and Busta Rhymes' "Get Out" blasted so loud the glasses jingled on their shelves. Jojo detached himself from the door frame and ambled among the remaining patrons, nudging reluctant guests toward the exit while the servers picked up empties and wiped down tables. Charlie stretched her aching feet and made a mental note to pick up some squishy insoles before tomorrow night's shift. Still, tonight was fun—a throwback to a simpler time when she'd been Bangers' most popular server. She missed those days when she could rely on warm greetings the moment she walked through her workplace door. So different from her mostly solitary work as a web designer.

The servers gathered at the bar to count out their cash tips while Dawn figured their share of the credit card totals.

"Seventy-seven, seventy-eight, seventy-nine..." Lana trailed off.

"Eighty, eighty-one, eighty-two." Rosie straightened her pile of bills.

"Eighty-three, eighty-four, eighty-five..." Aware of several pairs of eyeballs drilling her, Charlie lowered her voice and kept counting.

A thunk on the bar startled her into losing count. She glanced up to find River with arms crossed, lips pursed, glaring as if she were trying to get away with something.

"What?"

He tapped the beer mug before him. "Ten percent for the bartenders."

She regarded him coolly. "I'm aware. Worked here for fiveyears, remember?" While the other two servers counted out the bar staff's share, Charlie continued counting. "One oh one, one oh two, one oh three."

Kiara cocked an eyebrow and whistled. "Impressive. You pickin' pockets out there?"

"I'm engaging with my customers. Making them feel at home."

River snorted. "More like swishing her ass."

She straightened her shoulders. "Been watching my ass, have you?" What was this guy's deal, anyway? She hadn't done anything to earn his hostility, and she'd be damned if she'd let him get to her.

Dawn snatched up a damp bar towel, whirled it into a whip, and snapped it against River's flank. "Mind your business, mister. Charlie's doing me a favor—a big one. Plenty of bars on the Ave competing for customers. If our service is too slow, they'll try another bar, and that hurts my bottom line—yours too."

Rosie poked Lana and, giggling, gave her hips a shake. "Bottom line."

River sucked his teeth, turned away, and busied himself restocking clean glasses.

Charlie collected her jacket and bag from the break room and bid the other staffers good night. River glanced up, curled his lip, then went back to wiping the counter.

What the fuck? Sure, she had her faults, but—aside from her dad—she could usually pull a grin from most people she met. Why did this pretty boy take such an instant dislike to her? His problem, not hers, but his scorn stuck in her craw like a stinging hot pepper seed. She pulled her wooly scarf tighter around her neck and strode into the icy night.

Order *Christmas Rekindled*.

About the Author

Award-winning contemporary romance author Sadira Stone spins steamy, smoochy tales set in small businesses—a quirky bookstore, a neighborhood bar, a vintage boutique... Her stories highlight found family, friendship, and the sizzling chemistry that pulls unlikely partners together. When she emerges from her writing cave in Las Vegas, Nevada (which she seldom does), she can be found in dance class, strumming her ukulele, exploring the Western U.S. with her charming husband, cooking up a storm, and gobbling all the romance books. For a guaranteed HEA (and no cliffhangers!) visit Sadira at sadirastone.com.

Visit Sadira on All the Socials!

Also by Sadira Stone

Check out the rest of the swoony, steamy, laugh-out-loud *Bangers Tavern Romance Series*

Opposites Ignite: Bangers Tavern Romance 2

A mismatch sparks the hottest flames! Skinny, shy, strait-laced barback Eddie falls for curvy, tattooed, bodacious tattoo artist Rosie. Come to Bangers Tavern for steamy, opposites-attract romcom fun!

"I can't express how much I adored this story! The sweetest opposites attract, coworkers to lovers book with so much tenderness and major steam! I loved Rosie and Eddie and their families to pieces. A quick read with excellent pacing and so much cuteness you won't be able to put it down! Highly recommend!"
—Jess Hardy

Order *Opposites Ignite*

Delicious Heat: Bangers Tavern Romance 3

Cupid has lousy timing! Bangers Tavern chef Diego meets a woman who makes his heart sing. Trouble is, she's pregnant with another man's child. To win her, he'll have to convince her and both their interfering families that he's in it for keeps.

"The flavors jump off the page to soothe and incite the appetite. Then there's the steam which rises between Gogo and Anna from the moment they meet. This is a book about life, families—the good and the bad—and love which often comes when you least expect it.

On a scale of 1-5, *Delicious Heat* deserves a 7."
—Kat Henry Doran, Wild Women Reviews

Order *Delicious Heat*

Sweet Slow Sizzle: Bangers Tavern Romance 4

Bangers Tavern's hunky bouncer Jojo has been crushing on server Lana for years, but her sole focus is keeping her orphaned teen brothers together in the only home they've ever known. This slow burn, sizzling hot friends-to-lovers workplace romance celebrates the glorious chaos of 21st century family—the ones we're born into, and the ones we gather to our hearts.

"Sadira Stone writes gorgeous love scenes that are simultaneously physically arousing and emotionally moving. She does a wonderful job capturing the special intensity of sex with someone you truly love. I also really enjoyed the realistic portrayal of Lana's kid brothers. If only all teenage boys were lucky enough to have such a sensible and accepting big sister."
—Lisabet Sarai

Order *Sweet Slow Sizzle*

Check out Sadira's newest, ***The Trappers Cove Romance Series***

Welcome to Trappers Cove, a quirky Washington State beach town nestled among the pines. Here you'll find steamy, small-town romance, laughter and tears, Madame Zora's Psychic Emporium, all the best beachy fun, heart-warming chosen family, and guaranteed HEAs!

Passion in the Cards: Trappers Cove Romance 1

Headstrong, homebody farmer clashes with freedom-loving hippie chick, but their blazing chemistry is unstoppable. Though Jesse knows the bewitching fortuneteller Gemma will never settle down in their quirky beach town, he can't resist playing with fire.

"Among her many talents, author Stone shows readers and writers how to create two interesting and layered characters with everyday, relatable goals, motivation, and conflict, bringing all of it together in a novella length romance. Add in the steam and she's delivered another winner."
—Wild Women Reviews

Order *Passion in the Cards*

Passionate Brew: Trappers Cove Romance 2

When a control-freak brewery owner is forced to partner with a prickly master brewer, their business and their hearts will never be the same. Come to Trappers Cove for a sizzling enemies-to-lovers small town workplace romance.

"Ms. Stone writes wonderfully sensual prose, whether she's describing the crisp March breeze on an Oregon beach, the tartness of a cherry-flavored craft brew, or the smooth slide of skin against skin. *Passionate Brew* is an enjoyable visit to a special place. You may want to sit down, order an IPA and stay for a while."

—Lisabet Sarai

Order *Passionate Brew*

The Billionaire's Christmas Castle: Trappers Cove Romance 3

His billions can't buy what he craves most—her love. Can a spoiled tycoon and a fiercely independent entrepreneur cross an ocean of differences to forge a love that lasts past the holidays? Come to Trappers Cove for an Over-40 Christmas beach town billionaire romance that'll steam up your windows and warm your heart!

"I love that this story shows that sex and romance doesn't fade as you reach middle age! Sparks are immediate, and it's so much fun watching them fill in those pieces that they didn't know they needed from a partner in life."
—Myraffe

Order *The Billionaire's Christmas Castle*

Love, Legacy, and Little Green Aliens: Trappers Cove 4
Coming March 2024

Updating his late uncle's alien-themed souvenir shop is Xander's last chance to escape the family curse. Journalist Hannah vows to save the beloved landmark. Caught in a battle of wills and sizzling desire, they learn that Uncle Gus's UFO obsession was more than marketing. Come to Trappers Cove for a steamy rivals-to-lovers romcom full of found family, beachy fun, and out-of-this-world mystery.

Pre-order *Love, Legacy, and Little Green Aliens*

Cocktails from Bangers Tavern

♥

Still thirsty? Try these tasty cocktails mentioned in the story!

Pink Señorita

In a cocktail shaker, combine a shot of your favorite tequila (or more!) with pink grapefruit juice and simple syrup to taste. I like this drink on the tart side, but you may prefer a sweeter drink. Shake it up good, then strain into a tumbler filled with ice—or just use the ice from the shaker. Why waste good ice? Top your drink with a splash of cranberry juice, and garnish with fresh mint.

Green Demon

This one can be made in a glass or a pitcher, great for hot summer days! Combine equal amounts of Midori melon liqueur, vodka, and white rum—an ounce of each for a single serving, or multiply for a group. Stir it up, then add lemonade to taste, ice if you wish, and garnish with a slice of lime. Tasty and refreshing!

www.ingramcontent.com/pod-product-compliance
Lightning Source LLC
Chambersburg PA
CBHW061551310726
48972CB00008B/2703